THE WYLDES OF
CHELLOW HALL

1950s Yorkshire: Annabel journeys to her former workplace of Chellow Hall, home of the Wylde family. An unmarried mother, she has brought her baby Tommy — son and heir to one of the Wyldes — with her, feeling she should inform his father of the child's parentage. But disaster strikes when, near the Hall, she is knocked unconscious, waking later with amnesia. She has no memory whatsoever of her name, her reason for being there — or her son . . .

Books by Eileen Knowles
in the Linford Romance Library:

THE ASTOR INHERITANCE
MISTRESS AT THE HALL
ALL FOR JOLIE
HOLLY'S DILEMMA
FORGOTTEN BETROTHAL
ROSES FOR ROBINA

EILEEN KNOWLES

THE WYLDES OF CHELLOW HALL

Complete and Unabridged

LINFORD
Leicester

First published in Great Britain in 2017

First Linford Edition
published 2017

A catalogue record for this book is available
from the British Library.

ISBN 978–1–4448–3436–9

Published by
F. A. Thorpe (Publishing)
Anstey, Leicestershire

Set by Words & Graphics Ltd.
Anstey, Leicestershire
Printed and bound in Great Britain by
T. J. International Ltd., Padstow, Cornwall

This book is printed on acid-free paper

1

How did you inform a man he was a father, eight weeks after the event? Annabel leaned on the bridge parapet and sighed despondently. She'd thought and thought, but still had no satisfactory answer to that conundrum. Whatever she said, no matter how she tried to explain, she knew he wouldn't understand. How could he? She was still reeling herself from all that had happened in the last few weeks. What a shambles she had made of her life. The thing she regretted most, though, was that she had let her parents down. How disappointed they would have been if they knew of her predicament. But, on the other hand, it would never have happened if . . .

Not wanting to dwell on those unhappy thoughts, Annabel purposefully distracted herself by looking over the stonework, down into the turbulent water. Swollen by recent heavy rainstorms, what was normally a gentle, meandering stream had turned into a seething torrent of mud and debris. It surged and thundered angrily down to the now almost non-existent weir, where fallen branches marginally impeded its progress. She'd heard people on the train talking about the flooding in the area, and could clearly see a tidemark on the riverbank a good four feet above the present water level. Annabel marvelled at the unleashed, unrelenting power, and wished she didn't feel so weak and insignificant in contrast.

If only she had someone of her own age to talk to, she thought, wistfully. Someone who would understand what she was going through, and would listen to her side of the story, even if they couldn't actually do anything to help. Nobody else could. What was she to do to solve the problem? Not that she thought Tommy in any way a burden.

She loved her darling son. From the moment she set eyes on him she had been captivated, and vowed she would do all in her power to keep him healthy and happy. He was hers, all hers. The most precious thing she had in the whole, wide world. They belonged to each other, and since she had nobody else, no close relatives, he was so very, very cherished.

Why is life so complicated? she wondered, gazing at the brown, silty water, wearily brooding on how best to proceed with her intended obligation. Throughout the long, tedious journey, the problem had occupied her every minute. In fact, ever since Tommy was born — or, to be exact, from the moment she learned she was pregnant — it had concerned her greatly. She agreed, somewhat reluctantly, with the Palmers that the father ought to be told — indeed, had a right to be informed he had a son — and she should have done it earlier. Now she wasn't sure of anything.

Annabel was slowly reaching the conclusion that she shouldn't have come, and it would be kinder all round not to reveal to the Wyldes they had a son and heir. After all, Tommy was illegitimate, so wasn't exactly an heir himself to the Wyldes. She could manage somehow — alone. What if she found a live-in job somewhere as a domestic or nursery maid? She didn't think she would qualify as a house-keeper — her age would be against her — but kitchen staff was a possibility. If absolutely necessary, she supposed she could return to London and maybe get her old job back at the library, in which case she would have ready-made babysitters in the Palmers. Now Mr Palmer had retired it would give them an interest, and they were totally dependable, as well as being extremely charitable. Hadn't they taken her in when her parents were killed in the bombing raid, when other, unfeeling, far-flung relatives hadn't wanted to know?

She gave a monumental sigh. Life had been chaotic to, say the least, since just before Christmas when she learned she was seven months pregnant. It had come as an enormous shock. Stunned and terrified, she had turned to the Palmers as the only people she knew who would help her. They were the nearest she had to family. They looked on her as the daughter they never had, for which she would always be exceedingly grateful. She knew that, but for their generosity, she would have been sent to a children's home when her parents were killed. She had only been twelve years old at the time, a studious, shy child, and the thought of being incarcerated with lots of other unruly children would have been horrendous. They saved her from all that, thank goodness, and had been truly marvellous substitute parents.

She wished oh, how she wished! — that she had never met Jonathon Wylde. If they hadn't met, she would never have applied for the job and ended up working for his father, Sir Robert. It was fate, pure fate, but there was no point in railing about what had happened. That was the past and she had no one else to blame but herself. It had been her choice to visit Scarborough to try to locate distant relatives, and there Jon Wylde had nearly run her down. They got talking, and when he learned she was a librarian, he immediately suggested she meet his father who was looking for someone to catalogue his book collection. One thing led to another, and Annabel had spent over a year at Chellow Hall, working in the library and occasionally looking after Sir Robert and Lady Jane's daughter, Sophie. Sophie was lively and a bit of a handful, and the numerous nursemaids they employed didn't stay long, so Annabel had often filled in.

Looking back, she recollected how she had thoroughly enjoyed her time at Chellow Hall, and would have been delighted to remain there. It had been quite an awe-inspiring experience to begin with, though. When Jon transported her to Chellow Hall she thought she had never seen anything so imposing, and was completely intimidated by its grandeur. Latterly, she had grown to love it, until . . . She hadn't had the slightest suspicion of her pregnancy. She hadn't missed a period or felt unwell. She hadn't put on weight or gone off her food. There had been nothing to give her an inkling of her condition. Only when Lady Jane insisted she saw the doctor because she had 'flu-like symptoms, and she didn't want her darling Sophie infected, did the truth come to light. Annabel nearly fainted with shock, and her first impulse was to escape, escape somewhere, anywhere. She just wanted to hide. In the event, she simply informed her employers she'd had upsetting news from London, and told them she needed to extend her Christmas holiday indefinitely, to which they reluctantly agreed. They were a bit annoyed though, because they had hoped she would be at Chellow Hall for Christmas to be available to look after Sophie.

Annabel had headed south feeling sick with worry. The Palmers were expecting her to spend Christmas with them, but were surprised when she arrived so early. Annabel realised they would have to be told of her condition. She had to tell someone. She needed help and she had no one else to turn to. She wasn't sure what their reaction would be, and was prepared for them to show her the door. But, after their initial show of disapproval, they had been absolutely marvellous, and rallied round like excited grandparents. They had even provided her with the ancient pram which they had had stored in their attic. Apparently, they'd lost their only child at five months, and couldn't bring themselves to part with her things.

They had always told her she was welcome in their home any time. They had been good friends of her parents and had always taken a neighbourly interest in Annabel. She could return to London, and she knew they would do all they could to help, but could she expect it of them at their age? Would it prove too much? The responsibility of looking after a small baby was not something to take on lightly, even though they were both in good health as far as she knew. It would be an imposition, perhaps stretching neighbourliness to its limits. When she'd left, she hoped she had convinced them everything would be alright, having agreed the father should be informed and made to at least take some responsibility for Tommy's upkeep. In reality, she knew she couldn't foist the knowledge of his baby onto his father. For a start, Jon was recently married. She dreaded to think what his new wife would say if she ever found out. She could talk to Sir Robert, she supposed, but he had his own concerns — worrying health problems. So what was in Tommy's best interests? He was her real concern. He was all that mattered. How could she best give him the sort of life he deserved? Money wasn't everything — Annabel knew all too well that a loving home life was far more important than sumptuous surroundings — but you did need money to survive.

This was, in reality, a wasted journey. Now she was in the grounds, within striking distance of her objective, what in London had seemed outwardly sensible now felt nigh-on impossible. The Wyldes of Chellow Hall were nobility: people looked up to them, and scandal wouldn't go down well in this respectable, pious, rural community. Besides, she couldn't tell the father, thereby ruining his prospects of a happy marriage. No good could come of informing him about his son, even if Tommy proved eventually to be the heir to the Chellow Estate.

Annabel felt so desperately tired. Was it really only eight hours since she'd left London? Eight long, gruelling hours they had been. The trains were jam-packed — even the one from York to Scarborough. The one from London having been delayed, with the inevitable missed connection as a result, led to a lengthy wait, then twice as many passengers squeezed into too few carriages. Tommy, fortunately, was a placid baby, and slept a good deal of the journey, but Annabel had been too overwrought to sleep, despite being bone-weary. Mercifully, the train to Whitby had been relatively quiet, so she'd managed to doze in the corner of the carriage, until being abruptly woken by a ticket collector as the train exited the tunnel at Ravenscar.

The walk from the train had cleared her head, but it had been a long trek, not helped by the bitingly cold wind blowing straight in off the stormy North Sea. It could even snow. In fact, it was a strong possibility. It wasn't unknown for it to snow here in late February, apparently, so she should have worn boots. It was strange how different everything seemed in Yorkshire compared to the London streets.

Annabel sighed again, looking towards the pram as Tommy started to whimper. She would somehow have to manage on her own. There wasn't quite the stigma attached to being an unmarried mother like there used to be, thank goodness. This was the fifties, and since the war, women were becoming much more liberated — or so she'd heard. Tommy should be her responsibility, hers alone. Other women managed to bring up children without assistance from the father, and so could she if she put her mind to it. After all, she had made the decision to keep Tommy without consulting Jon, so why should he be expected to contribute for his upkeep? He could eventually have legitimate children with Patsy who would inherit — that was, if Lucas and Roxanne failed to produce offspring, as seemed the case.

Jon might try to persuade her to have Tommy adopted, which was something she would never entertain. Never in a million years would she give up Tommy.

She would rather scrub floors from morning until night if that were the only way they could survive. Then again, perhaps Jon wouldn't believe Tommy was his son. That thought sent a shudder through her. Why hadn't she thought about that before now? She had no proof to offer him, and only time would tell if Tommy bore any resemblance to him. It would be no good saying she had never been with any other man before or since. She just knew he wouldn't believe she had been a virgin.

'Oh, damn, damn, damn the lot of them!' she cried, pulling at the locket on the fine gold chain. It was the only present he'd ever given her, and second-hand at that. It broke at the clasp, and without giving it a second glance, Annabel strode to the centre of the bridge and hurled it into the river. For a moment it caught on an overhanging branch before trickling down into the swirling water.

She felt calmer now the decision had

been made. It was for the best, she knew it was. In truth, she had known it all along. The Palmers were trying to help, but they didn't know what she was up against. They couldn't possibly understand, never having left their closely-knit area of London where they had lived all their sheltered lives. Chellow Hall was another world. It was time to face facts. She needed a roof over her head, and to earn an honest living in whatever way she could: both of which she could achieve with the right attitude and commitment. First things first. It was beginning to get dark, so she ought to be heading back to Whitby to find a room for the night. Then tomorrow she would start looking for a job in earnest. She would take any job available. All she wanted was a roof over her head and to keep her darling son.

She heard a vehicle approaching. Coming at speed. *Lady Jane, no doubt*, thought Annabel, hugging the side of the narrow bridge, glad she had left the pram at a safe distance. Lady Jane was not the world's best driver by all accounts, and it was too late to find anywhere safer. It was a shame she should encounter her now, just when she had decided to return to Whitby and to leave the Wyldes in peace. She hoped Lady Jane wouldn't recognise her and maybe offer her a lift. That would prove rather awkward. She had just time to hoist herself on top of the parapet before the car swerved round the bend and skidded to a halt. It was only then that Annabel saw the horse and rider galloping along the near side. They had been neck-and-neck — clearly a race between Mrs Roxanne Wylde on her fiery mount, Demon, and Lady Jane in her husband's cherished sports car. Annabel wondered if Sir Robert had given his wife permission to use it, or was this another of the madcap exploits for which these two were renowned.

Seeing Annabel, the startled horse reared up, nearly unseating Roxanne.

At the same time, Lady Jane jammed on the brakes, slewing the car round, narrowly missing the end of the stone wall. In the ensuing mêlée, one of the horse's hooves clipped Annabel, sending her tumbling over backwards.

It happened in the blink of an eye. Too dazed to save herself, Annabel plummeted into the river. She struck her head on a protruding coping stone which fortunately numbed her senses as the icy water, that only moments before she had been studying with such awe, dragged her down. Self-preservation kicked in. Instinctively, she struggled against the surging current, trying desperately to keep her head above the surface, while gasping for breath from fear and the freezing conditions. Her duffel coat was like a lead weight, seemingly intent on drowning her, but she couldn't spare a hand to undo the toggles to slip out of it. It took all her strength to stay afloat as she thrashed her arms and legs about in befuddled panic.

The current carried her swiftly downstream, yet it seemed an eternity before somehow she made it to the riverbank close by the weir. Here, it was less deep, and her feet touched the bottom. At last, she managed to undo the coat, and it immediately floated over the weir before she had chance to save it. Grasping hold of a large, trailing branch, she succeeded with superhuman effort in scrambling up the muddy embankment, and collapsed in a grassy hollow where exhaustion claimed her.

How long Annabel remained there, she did not know. Time had no meaning as she drifted in and out of consciousness. She felt so tired . . . weary and sleepy. She floated effortlessly in a small boat through down-soft, cotton-wool clouds, until rudely awakened by a man bending over her, poking her roughly.

'Hey, you there. You all right?' His voice was sharp, tinged with exasperation, and he had to shout to be heard above the commotion as the swollen river cascaded over the weir, dragging debris along with it. 'You'll catch your death of cold like that. You can't stay here.' He stepped back as if undecided what to do, and looked down at his scruffy boots seeking inspiration. Then his gaze wandered off down the riverbank towards the bridge. Shrugging his shoulders, he appeared to be signalling to someone.

Annabel, back in the land of the living, struggled to sit up, staring at him in bewilderment. Before she could ask where she was, a violent attack of shivers beset her. She couldn't stop shivering. She had never felt so cold in all her life. Her clothes clung to her slim body like a second skin, and somewhere she had lost one of her shoes. She glanced around rather desperately. Something was wrong — very wrong — but she wasn't sure what. Fingering the wet hair plastering her face, Annabel feverishly pulled it back, as if by doing so she could restore some order to her haphazard thoughts.

Where was she? Who was she? Why was she so wet? What was she doing there?

'Want a hand?' the man asked, reaching out towards her. He'd come to a decision, but he looked none too happy about it.

Hugging herself in a vain effort to get warm, Annabel's expression was of blank indifference. She remained where she was. It could be a nightmare, except she felt so cold, and the man looked real enough. What had she done to make him so angry?

Comprehending Annabel was in need of help, the stranger, without asking a second time, bent down, and with a struggle scooped her up into his arms. She offered no resistance. She was past caring what happened to her. If only she could get warm . . . Courageously, the man staggered along the slimy path, slipping and sliding precariously near the edge of the water. His feet squelched with every step, his breathing becoming increasingly laboured. Sharply, he told her to hang on, which Annabel obeyed somewhat cautiously. He was no young-ster, and not particularly handsome. He smelled of stale sweat and unpleasant tobacco residue. No Prince Charming, obviously. With a sigh, Annabel gave herself up to his ministrations, hoping that before long some light would be shed on her situation.

When they neared the bridge, he called out to a woman she took to be his wife. 'Come and give me a hand for goodness' sake, Iris, she's heavier than she looks.'

Between them they hustled her over the bridge, along a rough track and into their farm cottage. Annabel was relieved to see a smouldering log fire and made a beeline for it. The woman threw on some small twigs, making it blaze, while the man disappeared, muttering something about a change of clothing.

'You'd best get out of those wet things,' the woman said, turning to Annabel with an exasperated look. 'I'll fetch you a blanket.'

Annabel was unable to do anything but shiver uncontrollably. She felt incapable of reasoned thought or action, but it was wonderful to feel the warmth of the fire. She stretched out her hands to the flames, oblivious to the steam rising from her clothes or the sparks leaping out from the crackling timber. The woman returned and immediately took charge, hurriedly peeling off Annabel's wet clothes and heaping them in the hearth. All the while she was muttering about how stupid Annabel was, and the state she was in. Finally, wrapped in a coarse woollen blanket, Annabel was settled in an armchair.

'You stay there and keep warm,' the woman said bluntly, as if speaking to a disobedient child. 'I don't know, you youngsters. Got no sense at all have you?'

Annabel shook her head cautiously. She couldn't remember anything — not a thing — not even her name. 'Name?' she said, questioningly.

The woman frowned. 'I'm Mrs Peters, of course — Iris Peters. You remember me? I work at the Hall. That's where we met.' Seeing Annabel's growing agitation, she went on slowly. 'Can't you remember anything?' She looked deeply puzzled, but then half-smiled reassuringly. 'Don't worry. It will be all right soon enough. I expect you banged your head or something. These things take time. I'll just warm up some soup.'

She disappeared into the kitchen tut-tutting, leaving Annabel thoroughly bewildered. She lay back feeling panicky. Who was she? Where was she? What was her name? She ought to be able to remember her own name, for heaven's sake!

2

'What do you mean, she's got amnesia? She can't have.'

'I'm sorry, Mrs Wylde, but it appears Annabel can't remember anything, not even her own name.'

Iris Peters stood by the side of the settee in the small sitting room the family often used for afternoon tea, and waited with arms folded. *Let's see how you get out of this*, she thought smugly. There wasn't just Annabel to deal with, but the baby too. Quite a pickle these two Wyldes had got themselves into — not for the first time, and sure-fire it wouldn't be the last. She realised Lady Jane was possibly the more compassionate and sensible of the pair, but was far too easily led astray by the wayward Mrs Roxanne. Roxanne Wylde, on the other hand clearly lived up to her name. Her pranks were getting more and more outrageous, and she wondered why her husband, Lucas, put up with her.

Roxanne got up from the armchair where she had been lounging and strode over to the window. 'The stupid, stupid girl,' she muttered, more to herself than the other occupants of the room. Fingering her forehead, she heaved a monumental sigh. Whatever happened, Luke must not hear about it. He had threatened to cut her allowance if he heard of any more shenanigans. Turning abruptly, she screamed, 'We can't be held responsible for what happened to Annabel Masters. What was she doing on the bridge in the first place, I'd like to know? It was her frightening Demon that caused the accident, so it was her own silly fault. If I hadn't had my wits about me, I might have had a very nasty tumble . . . like that neighbour fellow, Joseph what's-his-name, who they say will never walk again. I could easily have fallen in the river too. I tell you, the girl has a lot to answer for.'

Jane bit her lip, feeling guilty. What Roxanne said clearly wasn't true. They shouldn't have been racing about the grounds, and Annabel had every right to be at Chellow Hall.

Robert had been asking only the previous day when she would be returning. He was getting anxious about the state of the library. She replaced her cup and saucer carefully on the trolley. 'But if . . . '

Roxanne, in full flow now, turned her scathing fury in her direction. 'It was her own fault, I tell you, Jane. We didn't do anything to precipitate her fall. Annabel should never have been there.' Once she had shut Jane up, she grasped the back of a chair and breathed deeply. Having reached her decision, she snapped, 'We have to decide what to do with her, and I suppose as usual you expect me to come up with some solution.' Chewing a fingernail, she frowned thoughtfully for a moment. 'Is Robert expecting her back right now?'

Jane shook her head, desperately

trying to think. 'Annabel left before Christmas saying she had family matters to attend to. We didn't know when she would be returning, but . . . '

'There!' said Roxanne, brusquely washing her hands of the affair. She returned to her seat and calmly poured herself another cup of tea. 'I told you we can't possibly be held responsible, since Annabel wasn't in our employ at the time of the accident. In fact, we could accuse her of trespassing. There are far too many people walking willy-nilly on our land. We'd be bankrupt in no time if we had them all suing us for any minor mishap. Just send her packing, and the child too.'

Iris Peters stood patiently waiting, trying not to show her distaste at the behaviour of these two parasitic women. She had been left to deal with the situation they had precipitated. They hadn't even had the courtesy to wait and see if Annabel was all right. She had heard Lady Jane suggest doing so, but Mrs Wylde overrode her by reminding her of the time, saying they were late already, so they had both scampered off. And the only thing they were probably late for was afternoon tea! What a pity Sir Robert and Mr Lucas weren't there. If Sir Robert only knew what was going on . . .

Jane sighed and shuffled to the edge of her seat. She hated confrontations with Roxanne, but sometimes she just had to say her piece. Roxanne shouldn't be allowed to run roughshod over people the way she did and get away with it. Steeling herself, she said defiantly, 'We can't turn her out with nowhere to go, the state she's in.'

'Why not?' Roxanne retorted with her mouth full of scone.

'Oh, Roxy, for goodness' sake, it's obvious we have to do something. We have a responsibility. There's the baby to consider, for one thing. It is Annabel's, I presume?' She looked at Iris Peters for confirmation.

'Annabel doesn't know about the baby. I didn't think she was in any fit state to see it. I was fearful she might catch pneumonia, so thought it best to keep them apart. She hasn't mentioned the baby at all, so I'm not sure how best to proceed. All I know is, one shouldn't do anything too disturbing to alarm her in any way. I think, if you don't mind my saying so, it might be prudent to put Annabel in her old room here at the Hall. It might gently jog her memory back.'

Roxanne's nostrils flared. 'You presume too much. You have room at your place, don't you, Peters? You look after her, and the baby too, if you are so concerned for their well-being. Let us know when she's fit to travel and we can be rid of her. The sooner the better.'

Iris Peters, accepting this as her dismissal, shrugged her shoulders and turned to go. She could hardly bear being in the same room as the pair of them.

'No, wait,' Jane said, once again defying her sister-in-law. 'I think it would be best just as you say, Mrs Peters. Annabel's room is not being used at the moment. We can all keep an eye on her, see she comes to no harm — but maybe you should look after the baby, though. The fewer people aware of it, the better, for the time being — until we know a little more about the situation. If, in fact, it is Annabel's; and why she was bringing it here . . . ' She walked towards the door that Iris Peters opened for her. 'Give it a day or two, and then we'll see what else we need to do. This amnesia thing might be only temporary, and in a couple of days Annabel will be right as ninepence. Let us know what you need in the way of baby clothes and other necessities, won't you? I have some of Sophie's you can have.'

Iris Peters had known it all along. She'd told her husband Mrs Wylde and Lady Jane wouldn't want news of their escapade to get out, so he'd best keep his mouth shut. As she was about to leave, she said, 'What am I to say . . . ?'

'Oh, for heaven's sake; use your common sense, woman, and say Annabel has had a nervous breakdown or something,' snapped Roxanne. 'But don't you dare mention the baby. I don't want to hear the servants gossiping and spreading rumours about its parentage. Well, what are you waiting for?'

3

Annabel. *Annabel*. Her name was Annabel Masters. 'Annabel,' she said repeatedly, hoping for a spark of recognition, but nothing revealed itself. Yet it must be her name, because Iris Peters recognised her and said so, so why didn't it ring any bells? Her mind was as blank as a clean slate, her past a complete mystery. According to Iris, she was twenty-one or possibly twenty-two years old, and had worked at the Hall for over a year, employed by Sir Robert personally. She had supervised Sir Robert and Lady Jane's three-year-old daughter, Sophie, although was employed initially to catalogue the library at Chellow Hall. That was what they'd told her, so she supposed it must be true. Iris said she had always been a very private person and didn't say much about herself — too wrapped up in books to be sociable! *Stuck-up, she means*, Annabel thought with a wry smile.

Annabel spent long hours looking at herself in the dressing-table mirror, hoping for some spark of recognition to manifest itself. Hazel eyes, pale complexion, freckles, shoulder-length fair hair — why didn't they register? After twenty-odd years they ought to be so familiar, but it could be a stranger staring back. *An ordinary one, at that*, she thought, glancing at her figure dispassionately.

Pulling back her shoulders, Annabel stuck out her chest, and thought that was her best attribute — her breasts were well rounded and substantial, something to be proud of. Nobody would call her a raving beauty, but she wasn't too repulsive. *Passable* was perhaps the word that best described her, she thought — and maybe *homely*.

For the time being, she relished the solitude of her room and rarely left it, not wanting to make contact with others whom she should know but didn't recognise. She knew the staff talked behind her back, and obviously thought her peculiar, but there was nothing she could do about it — she was an oddity. She may well be a being from another planet with no past, no present — and who knew what the future would bring? The future worried her the most.

Whenever Annabel thought about the future, she thought about Mrs Wylde — Roxanne Wylde, wife of Lucas, the eldest son. Mrs Wylde made her feel uneasy — spied upon, as if she wasn't to be trusted, and yet she didn't know why. Just because she couldn't remember anything about her past didn't mean she was untrustworthy. Although at the back of her mind lurked the horrible thought she had done something terrible — something so bad that she had no wish to regain her earlier life. Annabel had an idea amnesia could be somehow deliberate, because the person didn't *wish* to remember. Was that what had happened to her? All she knew was that the long sleepless nights hadn't provided her with an answer.

If she had her own possessions, they might prompt some recollection — but who knew where they were? All that had been recovered was a rucksack containing a change of clothing. Lady Jane had thoughtfully sent a selection of clothes, which Annabel could adapt to fit — they wouldn't have been her choice normally, but beggars couldn't be choosers. She was, to all intents and purposes, alone and penniless. No family and no friends. Her parents had been killed in the war, apparently, someone said. That was the sorry state of affairs she had to come to terms with. For days she'd racked her brains, but her mind was a dark empty void. Annabel remembered nothing prior to her meeting with the Peterses. Everybody was being considerate, especially Lady Jane, and Annabel suspiciously wondered why; but whenever she broached the subject of her past, they quickly changed to another topic.

Because they said she liked reading, Annabel had been given a selection of books, which she reverently placed on the shelves in the corner, arranging them in alphabetical order like in a library. She had found out something about herself — she liked an orderly existence. It was terrible not knowing anything else, so that scrap of information was stored away with due deference. The staff had been primed not to remind her of her past, saying it was best Annabel remembered for herself. She did hope it wouldn't be long. She hated the feeling of being so inadequate, and was scared of what would happen to her if her memory didn't return. Also, she was afraid for when it *did*, wondering what it might reveal. Whenever she asked what she had been doing there, they said if was best if she remembered for herself, and hurriedly changed the subject. It was all such a mystery.

4

'We have to talk,' Roxanne whispered to Jane as they left the breakfast table together. 'Meet me down at the stables in half an hour.'

'Something wrong?' asked Jane, not enamoured of visiting the stables at the best of times. She didn't like horses and they didn't like her. She didn't like the way they snorted and stamped their feet. Most of the Wyldes rode, unfortunately — some even took part in the hunt — but not Jane. She had tried once, in order to please her husband, but found the whole experience one she never wished to repeat.

'See you there,' Roxanne retorted, 'and don't be late. I have a plan to get us out of this mess.'

Jane hurried to complete her tasks and slipped out of the back door before Robert could ask where she was going.

She didn't want Robert upset, so the sooner they could deal with this awkward situation the better, but for the moment she couldn't see how it was ever going to be resolved. She cursed Roxanne for having such a hold over her, and inciting her into doing stupid things. Roxanne was always bored out of her skull and looking for trouble, while all Jane desired was peace and tranquillity. She wished she could avoid Roxanne more often, but it wasn't easy in such a household. It had been somewhat easier when Jon was home. Jon, the high-spirited, playful brother-in-law. She missed him. He was quick-witted and charming, not wicked and selfish like Roxanne, who cared for nobody but herself.

As she hurried through the rose garden and past the herb plot, she thought, not for the first time, what a strange family she had married into. She was younger than both her husband's sons — not that they seemed to mind. Luke had accepted her from the start, with a kind of sober, unruffled formality. Jon joked and teased her, saying he wished he'd met her first. Roxanne had shown barely concealed hostility from the beginning, obviously envious of her title. Yes, it was a real shame Jon had gone to live in France following his whirlwind marriage. She really liked him. He brought gaiety and liveliness to the house. She knew he could be irresponsible, and his father threatened many times to disinherit him if he didn't mend his ways. Robert despaired of him, and was mightily glad to have him wed.

Thinking about Jon brought to mind the recent letter Robert had received. Jon didn't sound very happy, considering he'd only been married a few months. At the time she hadn't expected the marriage to last long, but didn't expect trouble quite so soon. Patsy wasn't the wife she would have chosen for him. She was far too calculating and cold, even mercenary. Jon did need someone strong to control his frivolous spending, it was true, but a warm-hearted family and home-loving woman would have been more suitable. He would make a wonderful father one day, or so she hoped. She guessed Jon might be feeling homesick, so she had written him a long, inconsequential letter. She knew she would pine for England if it were her — though not be homesick for her own family she admitted ruefully. In that, Jon and Jane were alike.

She strode breathlessly into the tack room, in a way eager to learn what Roxanne had to say, but also fearful it would entail her in another deception or ruse. Why was life so complicated?

'Why couldn't we talk at the house?' she asked. The sooner she got this meeting over with, the better. If she had her way, she would never go anywhere near the stables. She found the place nauseating and repugnant. She hoped Sophie wouldn't want to ride when she grew up. She certainly wouldn't encourage her.

Roxanne, neatly turned out in riding coat and breeches, was in the process of berating a groom. Dismissing him brusquely, she turned on Jane. 'Isn't it obvious? Because I'm going riding, and I also wanted somewhere we won't be disturbed or overheard.' A second later, though, she stroked the horse's head and fed him a sugar lump, speaking his name soothingly and gently. Jane half-expected her to actually kiss the smelly beast. She had concluded some time back that Roxy thought more of animals than humans, perhaps because they didn't answer back. She always did like to be in control.

'We have to decide what we are going to do with the baby,' Roxanne said, as calmly as if ordering a cup of tea.

'You mean Tommy?' said Jane, quickly stepping to one side to avoid coming into contact with the horse. ''Tommy' was embroidered on the front of his blue top, remember?'

'Tommy.' Roxanne grated her teeth, clearly hating the name. 'Yes, Thomas, who else would I be meaning? Sophie could hardly be called a baby, now, could she? Well, I've given it a lot of thought, and come to the only sensible conclusion — we'll adopt it. That is, Luke and I will adopt it.'

Jane gasped. Her eyes were on stalks. 'What! You can't . . . I mean, why?'

'Use your common sense, Jane, or what little brain you were born with. As you know, Luke and I have already discussed adoption.' She paused, biting her lower lip. 'Luke wants . . . needs an heir, dammit, and since I can't give him one — well. This baby is obviously the product of one of the men here on the estate. Why else was Annabel coming back here? She's such a little mouse of a thing, the father must be someone hereabouts.'

Jane was having difficulty breathing due to the enormity of what Roxanne was proposing — and she seemed so callous about it, too. 'I suppose it's possible,' she managed to wheeze, the claustrophobic atmosphere eventually getting to her. 'I hadn't thought . . . '

'Well, to me it's as plain as a pikestaff — he's probably a Wylde. You've only got to look at the colour of his hair to see that. All the male Wyldes have red hair. The only question is, which Wylde is the father?'

Jane unthinkingly collapsed onto a straw bale. 'That's unbelievable. Robert wouldn't . . . '

Roxanne laughed scornfully. 'Don't you believe it. All men are the same, given half a chance. Robert might be losing his sight, but that doesn't stop him wanting to prove himself in other ways, I bet.' Roxanne smirked, making Jane blush. 'I wouldn't even put it past Lucas either, knowing how badly he wants a son and heir. He could be scattering his wild oats. I suppose it could be Jon's, but now he's gone abroad we'll have to discount him. I've been trying to think about any other Wyldes that were here late last spring. We had quite a gathering for Robert's birthday, if you remember, and I

42

especially recall that randy Uncle Cameron making eyes at Annabel. He could be the father.'

Jane shook her head, struggling to grasp all the implications. If Tommy were a couple of months old now, that would make it somewhere about . . . 'It could be anyone on the estate. Just because he's got . . .'

'What I'm proposing is that Luke and I adopt this baby,' Roxanne said, somewhat belligerently, proceeding to lead Demon outside. 'It's the only rational solution. Thomas James, I think I'll call him. James, after my father.'

Jane, glad to escape the confines of the stable block, trotted out in front of them. 'But . . . but what happens when Annabel regains her memory? She'll know who the father is, and . . . well, I just think the whole idea is insane. You can't just ride roughshod over someone like that, Roxanne. We're talking about Annabel's life. Besides, we haven't told her yet about the baby. Maybe when she sees him she'll recover, and all will be well. It could be just what she needs to restore her memory. I keep telling you, but you won't listen.'

For days they had disagreed about whether Annabel was fit enough to learn she had a child. Jane had wanted to take the baby to show her, since Annabel kept saying she felt fine and was itching to do something useful, but Roxanne was dead against it. Now she knew why. Jane had secretly thought about disobeying Roxanne, but hadn't managed to summon up the courage, knowing she would have to face the full onslaught of her wrath if she did so. *If only I had more confidence*, she thought. Little had she realised what she was letting herself in for when she married Robert. She hadn't just married *him*, but the entire complex, bewildering Wylde family. She loved her husband dearly and would do anything to make him happy, even if it meant coping with his wayward daughter-in-law.

Roxanne stood facing Jane now,

slapping her boots with her riding whip. 'That, my dear Jane, is why Annabel must not see him. Never, do you understand? Strange as it may seem, I want to preserve my pretence of a marriage, and this is a heaven-sent way of doing so. Obviously Annabel wouldn't be in any position to look after the child. How could she? She's a penniless nobody. She was clearly on her way to confront the father and make demands when she had this unfortunate accident. I'll be doing her — them both — a favour. Save us all the scandal into the bargain.'

'What do you mean? We can't . . . '

'I mean, we send her away.'

It was a nightmare. Jane closed her eyes and wished . . . *wished* she could coax Robert into living at their Spanish villa. It would be much more convenient now his eyesight had deteriorated to such an extent that he had more or less handed over the running of the estate to Luke. She could get away from Roxanne and her stupid goings-on, and it would be so marvellous for Sophie. She pictured the three of them enjoying life in the sun, away from the never-ending problems of running such a large property — and, of course, escaped from Roxanne's influence.

Luke could manage; in fact, he would probably prefer to have hold of the reins without interference, Jane surmised. Roxanne wouldn't, though. She said she hardly saw Luke as it was, so if Robert left, he'd have even less time to spend with his wife. Roxanne was always moaning about how she had to attend events alone because Lucas pulled out at the last minute. Not that Luke liked the social scene, from what Jane had observed. He made an effort to appease his wife and venture out when necessary, but often looked ill-at-ease amongst Roxanne's so-called friends. She wondered why such an ill-matched couple had decided to marry in the first place. For Roxanne, it was prestige, no doubt. Luke? Well, who knew? Roxy probably went all-out to snare him, and he was trapped before he realised what was going on . . .

Whatever the reason, that was their problem. Jane had her own difficulties to deal with. Being Robert's second wife, it hadn't been easy trying to live up to the standard set by the Wyldes. Roxanne was always getting her into scrapes, but this was the worst ever. Jane wanted nothing to do with it, but on the other hand she couldn't see any alternative. Roxanne was right in that Annabel would find life terribly hard trying to bring up the baby as an unmarried mother. On the other hand, if ever Sophie were taken away from Jane, she would go out of her mind. Sophie wasn't the easiest of children to cope with, but she was her daughter. Jane loved her intensely, and suspected Annabel would feel the same about Tommy.

'Where would Annabel go?' she said with a sigh. Roxanne always got her own way, so what was the point of arguing?

'Luke's Uncle Percy. He sent his last housekeeper packing a couple of months ago, and you know he's too old to be living alone. Annabel will be an ideal companion. She always said she liked isolation, so what could be better?'

'Uncle Percy,' gasped Jane. 'But he lives in the middle of nowhere, and he's . . . well, to tell the truth, I'm not sure he's all there.'

'So? That makes it even better, don't you think?'

Jane sighed. Poor Annabel. Not only was she never to know the joy of bringing up her son, but also was to be sent to the wilds of the Yorkshire Moors to become housekeeper to a slightly loopy old man. She wanted to protest and say she would have nothing to do with it, but she knew Roxanne would involve her whatever happened.

With shoulders drooping, she turned and walked back to the house, deep in thought. Earlier, she had made up her mind to come clean — to talk to her husband and reveal all her misdemeanours. Then maybe she would feel competent to rebuff Roxanne's outrageous schemes. Jane knew she should have done so from the outset, but now things were getting out of hand. Roxanne was becoming just too unbearable for words. She would choose her moment . . .

What finally tipped the scales was the letter that arrived by the second post. It was addressed to Robert, but fortunately Jane dealt with most of his post these days, only handing him those of any consequence. As soon as Jane saw it, her heart sank. First, the London postmark made her apprehensive, then she thought she recognised the handwriting. She felt physically sick, so went into the library and sat down. Nervously slitting open the envelope she paused, determined that, whatever the problem, she would cope. She began reading, breathed a great sigh of relief when she discovered it wasn't from whom she'd first thought, but then gulped at the realisation that things were not so simple as Roxanne had anticipated.

Dear Sir,

   Annie Masters has been like a daughter to us since her folks were killed. She set out more than a week ago to see you. We haven't heard from her and we are getting worried for her safety. Please could you let us know if she arrived and all is well? We don't want to interfere, but after all that has happened to her recently we'd like to know she is all right.
   Much obliged,
   Daisy Palmer

'Something interesting, my dear?' Robert asked.

Jane nearly jumped out of her skin. She had been so engrossed in the letter, she hadn't heard her husband enter the room.

'No,' Jane murmured, re-reading the letter with mounting apprehension. 'No

. . . Nothing I can't deal with.' Getting to her feet, she kissed him on the cheek. 'I shall be going into Whitby later to do some shopping; is there anything I can get for you?'

As soon as Jane could catch Roxanne on her own, she showed her the letter. 'What are we going to do?' she wailed. 'These people are missing Annabel. There might be others too.'

'Forget it,' Roxanne said with an imperious shrug of her shoulders.

Jane stared at her, dumbfounded. 'How can we? We have to reply.'

'Pretend we didn't receive it,' Roxanne snarled. 'Things do get lost in the post, you know.' Grabbing the offending paper, she screwed it up and threw it into the nearby fire. 'There, that's dealt with. Easy when you know how.' She strode off, leaving Jane incredulous.

Jane quickly tried to retrieve the remnants of the letter, but most of it had burnt. Fortunately, though, she had remembered the address, since it was not too far removed from where she used to live herself. How could Roxy be so intolerant? Jane knew better than most how concerned the Palmers would be. They might only be neighbours, but they were obviously caring people. Jane was touched by the simple request, and felt saddened at having to lie to them, but there was going to be no alternative.

Absent-mindedly, she crumpled the scorched fragments. What if . . . could Annabel . . . ? Flouting Roxanne's wishes for once, she pondered: what if she transported Annabel and Tommy back to London, and not to Uncle Percy's? Then what? The Palmers would want to know . . . no, Roxanne was right. What else could they do? At least Tommy would have a good home if Luke and Roxy adopted him, although Jane had doubts about Roxanne being a wonderful mother. Ever since Sophie was born, Roxy could hardly bear to be in the same room as her, let alone play with or cuddle her.

She worked on the principle that children should be left in the nursery until old enough for intelligent conversation.

Jane refrained from going into Whitby, and spent the rest of the afternoon concocting a reply she hoped would appease the Palmers. It was a very difficult letter indeed, and later that evening she decided she really must speak to her husband. She was about at her wits' end, and somehow had to summon up the courage to divulge her guilty secrets to Robert, desperately hoping he would understand. She knew she couldn't go on in her present state or she would be heading for a nervous breakdown.

5

'Robert, dear,' Jane said quietly. 'I have a confession to make. I hope you won't think too badly of me when you hear what I have to say.' He was sitting in his usual armchair glancing through a book of landscapes with the aid of a magnifying glass. Jane went to sit at his feet, needing to be close to him while she opened up her heart. 'I've been meaning to clear up a few . . . misunderstandings that arose . . . I didn't mean to mislead you. Honestly. It just . . . well, it just happened, and there never seemed an opportunity to rectify things.'

Robert stroked her shiny black hair, ruffling it playfully. 'Whatever it is, Janey, I forgive you.' He smiled and kissed the top of her head. He loved her dearly, and forever blessed the day they met.

'You don't know what I've done,' she whispered, and with a great sigh shook her head. 'I'm really not who you think I am, Robert. I'm not an orphan, and I'm not from a middle-class background like I told you.' She gulped and hurried on. 'My parents are still alive. My father is . . . well, he works on the docks in London. They live in a ghastly little terraced property near the river, and I hated it.' Turning to look up at him, she continued bravely, explaining: 'Can you imagine rows and rows of pokey houses with no front gardens and only a small back yard to hang the washing out? The walls were so paper-thin one could hear the neighbours arguing day and night, and I had to share my bedroom with my two younger sisters. I honestly couldn't wait for the day I could make my escape.'

Realising Robert didn't seem too upset, but had merely closed his book and was listening intently, she continued. 'As soon as humanly possible, I left that wretched district to make a better life for myself. Was I wrong,' she sobbed, 'to want a nice place to live, pretty clothes and a beautiful home? Maybe you think so. Maybe you think I have deceived you? I'm sorry if that is the case, but I do love you, Robert, really I do. I didn't marry you because you were rich and influential. I truly wanted to make you happy. I thought I could do so. I felt . . . I felt . . . I still feel there is something magical between us. From the moment we met, I knew you were the only man I'd ever want to marry.'

Robert caressed her cheek. 'Don't keep saying you're sorry, my love. You have and do make me happy. Extremely happy. Moreover, I'm not blaming you for your family background. How could I? It was you the person I fell in love with. One look at your ethereal face and I knew I had to get to know you better. I was — smitten, I believe the term is. In a way, I'm as much to blame as you, since I didn't ask you much about your family. I know I took you at your word, but . . . I felt sorry for you, yes, when you said you had no relatives, but as long as we had each other nothing else mattered.'

'And you don't mind . . . ?'

'My dear, now *I'll* let you into a secret. My first marriage wasn't the bliss everyone thought. It was what one would almost call an arranged marriage. Both families coerced us . . . it was our duty. Victoria needed the prestige of being a Wylde to be accepted by the county set, and my father assured me we needed the breeding stock that was part of her dowry. I had known Victoria most of my life — we grew up together, so it didn't seem too outrageous for us to marry. As it turned out, we didn't need the horses as our own stock turned up trumps, but by then it was too late.

'I wasn't exactly unhappy with Victoria. She gave me two fine, healthy sons, fulfilling her duties quite faithfully, but without much affection or passion. We rubbed along, displaying the right amount of endearment the public expected, but going our separate ways for much of the time. I escaped to the library when Victoria entertained her many friends. She enjoyed throwing cocktail parties and revelled in the hunting scene, which I could never abide, much as I like horses, as you know. As a marriage, it left a lot to be desired; and you, my dear, were instrumental in showing me what I had been missing.'

'Oh, Robert,' Jane gasped, momentarily relieved. 'I'm afraid there's more.'

'Tell me all,' he said softly.

Jane took a deep breath and dabbed her eyes. She settled on a footstool at his feet and held his hand. 'My parents never aspired to better themselves. Dad worked long hours doing manual labour down on the docks, and Mum took in sewing. She couldn't go out to work — not with five of us to look after. I knew that when I was old enough to leave school I was destined to work at the local clothes factory, like most of the women in our neighbourhood. There was never any question of my being able to go to university or anything. I was doomed to spend my life working for a pittance, which I would be expected to hand over to my parents so they could waste it down at the pub. That wasn't for me. There had to be a better way — a better life. I was determined to find an alternative.

'The day I left school, I packed what few clothes I possessed into a rucksack and headed north. I know that seems strange, and most young people make for the bright lights of London, but for me it was the opposite. I'd seen pictures of Yorkshire on a calendar in the newsagent's, and I thought it looked wonderful. All those charming fishing villages, the sandy beaches and rock pools, the wild barren moors and the magnificent historic houses with impressive gardens ... I daydreamed about them, but never ever thought I would actually live in such splendour. It was a fantasy, nothing more.'

Robert nodded, smiling gently, urging her to continue.

'I had very little money when I left — just pocket money which I'd secreted — but I've never begged or stolen from anyone in my whole life. I was determined to make my own way to better things through hard graft. I didn't mind what I did as long as it was honest. I caught the train to York and stayed in the railway station the first night. I remember it was a bit nerve-racking, being all alone in a strange place, and wondering what my parents would think when they got the note I had left them.

'I hid in the ladies' toilets for a long time, fearful someone would want to know who I was and what I was doing there. When it grew dark, I lay on one of the benches on the platform, feeling awfully alone and vulnerable, tired but too scared to sleep. At one point I nearly decided to catch the next train home, but when daylight eventually came I knew I had to stay and make it work. I couldn't go home without having made a success of my life. I wanted to show my family there is a better way of living if you try — if you really want it, of course.

'I felt my luck was in when very quickly I found work at a small café near the railway station. I had gone to buy a cup of tea to warm up myself up, and saw they had a vacancy for a waitress. It wasn't much of a place, but for some reason the owner took pity on me and let me doss down in his attic. The wages weren't great, but occasionally I was given a tip from a satisfied customer, and for me it was a start. My first job — first pay packet.'

Now that she had begun to relate her story, Jane felt easier. Knowing Robert wasn't cross about the deception, she recalled her earlier hardship almost as an adventure. 'You've no idea how wonderful I thought that pokey room was!' she said with a chuckle. 'It was my home — the first place of my very own where I could do exactly as I pleased. It was pure heaven. It was no bigger than your dressing room, but to me it was bliss. It had a cracked sink in the corner, and one ring to cook on where I heated up my beans on toast. That was my staple diet, beans on toast. I stayed there for nearly a year, but then unfortunately the café was sold and I had to move on. The new owners didn't need staff because they had family of their own. Next, I found work in a dress shop in the better part of town, and luck was again with me, as one of the other assistants wanted a flatmate. My guardian angel was obviously looking after me. I took it to be a step up in my career.

'I was only a very junior assistant, and spent most of my time clearing up, unpacking boxes and making endless cups of tea, but it was better-paid and I did enjoy it. Exquisite clothes, the like of which I could only dream about, surrounded me. One dress could cost more than a month's wages, and the customers — well, they were a revelation, I can tell you. I used to watch them strutting about, jewels dripping from their fingers, hair neatly coiffed, and faces made up to perfection. I thought — one of these days that will be me; all one needs is money.

'I tried to imitate the way those women walked, and the way they talked. In the privacy of my room I practised speaking more eloquently, picking up certain phrases that kept cropping up. I knew my accent let me down. People often remarked on it. They could tell where I came from as soon as I opened my mouth, and it made me feel ashamed. I soon realised that becoming a lady wasn't just about being able to speak properly, I had to look the part too. Like being an actress. I expect everyone laughed at me behind my back, but I didn't care. I had to better myself in the only way I knew how.

'That job didn't last long, and then I moved on to Madame Suzy's — a much smaller, but more exclusive, boutique. Madame Suzy was nice. She took me under her wing and trained me — let me serve some of the customers occasionally, and helped me in lots of little ways. She suggested ways to improve my appearance, and told me once I could have become a model — with the right training, of course. I really liked working there.

'Then, one day I was by myself in the salon — that was most unusual, but Madame Suzy had popped to the bank and the other assistant was off ill. This particular morning, one of our more affluent customers came in, all of a flurry. She desperately needed a gown for that evening, she declared, and had nothing remotely suitable in her wardrobe. I knew she had purchased several only recently, but I didn't let on. If I could satisfy her, I would get a commission, and it would be substantial because that particular customer only bought top-of-the-range models. I did my absolute best, and showed her all we had, but she was rather grumpy when she learned Madame Suzy wasn't there to fawn over her. She didn't care for being served by an underling. She knew I was only a trainee and looked down her supercilious nose at me.'

'Was that customer my wife Victoria, by any chance?' Sir Robert ventured, a smile lurking on his lips. 'I believe she spent a fortune at that particular salon.'

'Why, yes!' Jane chuckled. 'How clever of you to guess. Your wife was one of Madame Suzy's best and favoured customers. I used to think, *Fancy coming all the way from Chellow Hall to shop!* It's funny, really, but in those days I used to have to watch for Pettigrew arriving, and then I was expected to carry out the boxes and packages which he faithfully stowed away in the boot. To this day, I don't think he recognises me as that assistant. I was overwhelmed by the opulence of the car, and I used to dream that one day I too would live like that — buy gorgeous clothes, drive around in a super car, and have holidays in the sun. That has always been my goal in life.'

'You didn't consider marriage as a way of getting what you wanted?'

'No, never,' Jane said adamantly, waving her arm in the air. 'I thought life such as this was really way beyond my wildest hopes, just a mere daydream — but I liked to dream. Sometimes dreams are better than reality, don't you think? I'd heard of girls marrying rich men for their money, but strangely enough, I firmly believed I would remain single. I didn't fancy living the way my parents lived — never seeming happy, always arguing. I would rather remain single than be like that. It wasn't for me. And I didn't believe there was a knight in shining armour ready to rescue me from a life of drudgery. You must believe me, darling, I didn't purposely fall in love with you. It happened, and nobody was more surprised than me.'

'I know, my dear. For me too. I never expected a young slip of a girl like you would look twice at a staid old widower like me.'

'You are neither old nor staid, and it was my good fortune it was you I spilled the soup down.'

'Fate led me to that particular restaurant that night,' Sir Robert said with a wry grin. 'Go on with your story. I'm fascinated.'

Jane shuffled closer and smiled ruefully. 'Your wife wasn't easy to satisfy. To be honest, there was no pleasing her. I had shown her more or less every gown I thought remotely suitable, but none were acceptable. They were either the wrong colour or too ordinary, too gaudy or just plain inappropriate. I was at my wits' end and feeling out of my depth, so was greatly relieved when Madame Suzy returned. Your wife told her in no uncertain terms how totally incompetent I was, and wondered why I was retained in such a responsible position. I was mortified. I had done everything possible to please her. Nobody could have done more.

'Shortly after that experience, I'm afraid I was given my cards. Madame Suzy said it was because business was slow and she couldn't afford my wages, but . . . ' She shrugged her shoulders. 'That was just before Christmas, and I had been hoping to send my sisters some surprise presents with money I had saved, but it wasn't to be. Work was hard to find after that. So, with my money running out, I decided to hitch a lift to Scarborough, where I heard the hotels took on staff for the festive period. Unfortunately there were no vacancies, but I was told about a barmaid's job going in Whitby. I've worked as a chambermaid, a toy shop assistant, a nanny . . . finally, I got the job at the Crystal as a waitress. I had only been there a week when I met you, and you know what happened then.'

'It wasn't your fault that clumsy oaf nudged your arm and I ended up with soup in my lap.'

'The manager thought it was,' Jane

said glumly. 'If you hadn't insisted on telling him it wasn't my fault, he would have fired me on the spot. How I managed to finish my shift, I'll never know. I kept wondering where I would go if I lost that job. I would have been out on the streets with little money and no reference. I'd be back where I started. Life seemed so unfair. No matter how hard I worked, I never seemed to be able to hold down a job for long, or save much money. Anyway, I tried hard to discover who you were so I could thank you properly for putting in a good word for me, but none of the other waitresses recognised you — you weren't a regular, were you? At the time it happened, I was too flustered to do anything except wish the earth would open up and swallow me, and of course you were hustled away by the head waiter before I recovered from the fiasco . . . if that is the right word.'

'It will do,' he murmured cheerfully. 'I was in rather a mess, and I don't particularly like oxtail soup.'

Jane laughed for the first time in a week. 'When my roommate came and said there was a gentleman in the car park asking for me, I'm afraid I got panicky. I guessed it would be you, and I didn't know if I could face you.'

'I hope you didn't think I was wanting recompense of a different kind?' He chuckled.

'You were a perfect gentleman as always, my love. When I saw the limousine — I recognised it, of course, and thought how fitting it was that you had saved me from losing *this* job, when . . . maybe . . . well, I don't know. Anyway, I was thrilled to bits when you asked me out. I was dancing on cloud nine. I knew what most people would think — about . . . well, you and me, but I didn't care. I knew you were respectable and I had nothing to worry about on that score.'

Robert clasped her hand. 'Do you know, Jane, I was nervous as a schoolboy? It had been years since I'd asked a girl out, and I didn't know what

I would do if you turned me down. It was pure impulse. There you were, younger than my sons. I don't know how I had the audacity. When you said yes, I could hardly believe my ears.'

'I still can't believe my good fortune,' Jane said softly, tears glistening. 'My guardian angel was indeed working overtime that night. You truly are my knight in shining armour, Robert. You know that, don't you?'

Robert pulled her close. 'Where does that leave us, my poor little Cinderella? What can we do to help your family?'

'Nothing,' Jane retorted firmly. 'My family are not your concern. If you gave them money, they would only squander it — down at the pub, probably. I'm not being harsh, but realistic. They are content with their simple life, I can see that now, but it didn't suit me.' She gave a huge sigh. 'There is one other thing I have to own up to. A man I met . . . when I lived in York. He pestered me to go out with him, so I did — twice — but found him conceited and unpleasant. He didn't take kindly to being refused. However, one day a couple of years ago, I was out with Roxanne and we met him, quite by accident.' Jane paused and bit her lip, remembering how he'd made a play for Roxanne and she had flirted with him. 'He told a pack of lies about our relationship, but Roxanne believed him, and . . . and she's been sort of blackmailing me ever since. She said she'd tell you a story, embroidering it to such an extent that you wouldn't wish me to stay, and you'd demand a divorce. I do love you, Robert, and couldn't bear to leave. I know I'm not clever, and I haven't got Roxanne's looks or Patsy's social graces . . . '

'My, dear girl, why didn't you tell me all this before? You are far superior to either Roxanne or Patsy. You have nothing whatsoever to apologise for. You certainly have no need to show remorse for your upbringing. As for whatever tale Roxanne told, I would have taken it with a giant pinch of salt, because I know how wicked she can be. As Lucas's wife, we have to make allowances, but I can tell you in all honesty she is not the person I would have chosen for him. As for Patsy . . . well, Jon needs a strong woman to keep a tight rein on him. He's far too gullible and decadent, but then again, she's too much of a career woman for my taste. Not delightfully feminine like you, my pet.' He gazed at her tenderly and said softly, 'If truth be known, I've been afraid you'd be the one seeking a divorce. With me going blind . . . I've been on tenterhooks . . . '

'Oh, no!' Jane cried. 'No! I would never do that. I love you, and I . . . I just want us to be happy. If nothing can be done . . . if you *do* go blind, I'll do everything I can to help you. However, we'll cross that bridge when we come to it.' She gave a great sigh of relief. 'Please, Robert, do you think we could have a holiday? Let's go to Spain for a few weeks. It would be so nice to have time to ourselves, don't you think?'

He nodded. 'Yes, I think you're right. We deserve a break.'

'You know, in a way I love the villa more than I do Chellow Hall,' she added cautiously.

Robert raised an eyebrow.

'Strange, isn't it,' she continued. 'I always wanted to know what it would be like, living in one of these rambling old houses. I fantasised about all the servants, the elegant balls and extravagant gracious living, but it isn't like that at all. It's far colder and draughtier for one thing, and it's somewhat impersonal. Does that make sense?'

'I've lived here all my life, so I'm used to it,' Robert replied thoughtfully, 'but I understand what you mean — I think. It is a far cry from a two-up two-down, I expect.'

She smiled. He did understand. She thought about Annabel. In some ways, Annabel was fortunate not to have the burden of troubles from the past. Would she ever be able to escape her past? Well, she had made a start, and vowed she wouldn't let Roxanne dominate her ever again. She wished she could stop Annabel from going to Uncle Percy, but that wasn't something she could cope with right now. One thing at a time.

6

Annabel was to have travelled by bus to Holly Bush Farm, but at the last moment Lady Jane insisted on taking her, saying it was her duty to pay Uncle Percy a visit before the family went on holiday. Percy Wylde was one of Robert's distant cousins. He was an awkward cuss, often bad-tempered, antagonistic seemingly from pure devilment. He'd never married, and viewed women as pure domestics, fit only for being subservient to the male of the species. Jane knew Robert had tried to get Percy to sell up and stay at Chellow Hall, but the old man had refused point-blank. Jane wasn't sure if that was a good thing or not. Having him stirring things up at the Hall would only add to her problems.

She didn't relish the visit, but since the old buzzard wasn't in the best of health, and Annabel was to be seconded to him, she felt exceedingly guilty. Jane wanted to do all she could to smooth Annabel's relocation. She hoped it wouldn't be long before Annabel's memory returned . . . *But then what will happen?* she wondered. Roxanne hadn't thought her scheme through properly. One way or another, it was all going to come out, so Jane only hoped she wouldn't be around when that happened. The prospect of a long vacation in Spain was exceedingly welcome.

She told Annabel the chauffeur would take them both, setting off early one morning, but Jane would be returning the same day. She couldn't bring herself to consider staying overnight; and besides, she had packing to do. From what she recalled from her last fleeting visit to Holly Bush Farm, Annabel was going to have her hands full. It certainly wasn't going to be an easy assignment. Percy wasn't short of a bob or two, but lived very parsimoniously and despised waste of any sort.

Annabel was greatly relieved to learn she wasn't going to have to meet her new employer alone. The very thought frightened her to death. She was still bewildered by her loss of memory, and terribly anxious about the job, which apparently she had applied for and got without an interview. It was all so terrifying. Why couldn't she remember? Why had she wanted to leave Chellow Hall? Had she done something wrong? And what had possessed her to seek a job so far away? It was all so strange. She stared at the bleak countryside as the car effortlessly travelled the winding roads.

She was fascinated by the barrenness, and in some way found comfort in it. It looked so . . . desolate and solitary. Just like her. Perhaps that was why she had accepted the post. The position was that of Acting Housekeeper, Mrs Roxanne Wylde had informed her. It sounded rather grand, but wasn't she rather young to be a housekeeper?

They motored along narrow country lanes and through pleasant moorland villages for quite a while before Lady Jane spoke. 'Uncle Percy is a little unusual. Don't be surprised at some of his weird ways. He's harmless enough, though, I assure you.'

'I'll be fine,' declared Annabel, trying to sound more confident than she felt. 'I just hope . . . well . . . that I prove to be satisfactory. I'm not sure what the post consists of.' Annabel didn't know what she would do if he sacked her and turned her out. Where would she go? She felt panicky all over again.

'I'm sure you will be fine. It's just general housework. Nothing you can't cope with, I'm sure, but if — and I really mean this, Annabel — if you ever find you need a friend, I hope you will make contact with me. I think everyone should have someone they can turn to in an emergency. I can't even imagine what it must be like for you with nobody.'

Annabel nodded, wondering if Lady Jane had somehow read her thoughts, and couldn't help wondering why she was being so helpful. 'Does Mr Wylde live alone — I mean, is he a widower?'

'Oh yes, my dear, he lives quite alone, but I'm afraid he's the typical bachelor — never ever considered marriage, I understand. He's had a succession of housekeepers over the years, I believe. I don't think he has any other close relatives apart from my husband. Not that being a second cousin is so close, but Robert does feel sort of responsible for him. It would be far better all round if he lived at Chellow Hall, but he steadfastly refuses to do so.'

So, he had difficulty in keeping a housekeeper, did he? That answered one of her questions, then. Annabel wanted to ask lots of others, but decided not to do so. She was committed to the job, at least for the moment. She would just have to make the best of it. Surely it couldn't be too difficult looking after one man.

'We're nearly there,' Lady Jane said, fidgeting with her bag and gloves. They had just passed a clutch of houses near a church, and Annabel spotted the village shop. It looked rather quaint, and she guessed it sold everything from carbolic soap to locally grown vegetables.

About a mile further on, the car bounced down a rough track and pulled up outside an austere-looking stone farmhouse. There were no other properties within sight, just the grim stone building and a wide expanse of featureless moor. Annabel's heart sank; she hoped it would be more appealing inside, but somehow knew it wouldn't be.

There were no flowers in the front garden, just weeds, and the iron gate hung from broken hinges. She glanced cautiously at the windows. Tatty net curtains and peeling woodwork made her give an involuntary sigh, and she hopped out of the car before Pettigrew could assist her. This was nothing like

Chellow Hall. To the onlooker, it could even appear deserted and derelict. Lady Jane forced a smile of encouragement and marched up to the front door, with Annabel trailing in her wake, carrying a case containing her few possessions.

7

Roxanne sat in the elegant, though old-fashioned, drawing room waiting for Luke. He was late again, which meant the meal would be cold and inedible. He was always so damned busy these days. Ever since Robert and Jane left for their extended holiday in Spain, he'd become obsessed with work to the exclusion of all else. She'd thought that once they had the house to themselves, they could do lots more entertaining; get out more as a couple, live a little. She wanted to go to the theatre, have holidays, visit friends, go shopping in London . . . but she had been sadly mistaken. With Luke it was all work, work, work.

Roxanne sighed. Luke had greeted Thomas's arrival with genuine enthusiasm, and hadn't asked too many questions about his parentage, fortunately. She'd said something about the mother being unmarried, so unable to keep the baby, and it had been surprisingly easy to convince him the formalities could be completed at a later date. Normally he would have been a stickler for the appropriate paperwork being processed first, but he could see how much it meant to her so he had relaxed. Perhaps he thought Thomas would occupy all of her spare time, maybe wear her out so she wouldn't pester him quite so much. Well, *he* was sadly mistaken on that score. Motherhood was not something she could take to. She had cautiously tried to take an interest in the baby's upkeep, but found the whole thing revolting, messy and humdrum. She was glad to hand him over to the redoubtable Miss Grimshaw, and only handled him when she absolutely must. Luke liked to spend a few minutes each evening in the nursery, seeming to take an interest in Thomas's progress, so Roxanne feigned delight too, but at other times she stayed well clear.

Since Jane had left, though, she was often at a loose end, and more bored than ever with nobody to antagonise or distract her, so she had come up with a plan. As mistress of Chellow Hall — which, to all intents and purposes, she was — surely she could now have her way and modernise it. Jane had no flair for such things; and anyway, she accepted the *fait accompli* far too readily. Silly, stupid Jane was too naïve for her own good. She didn't seem to realise the power and influence she could wield. Robert obviously adored her — was besotted with her — so Jane could have anything she wanted. She would only have to roll those cat-like eyes, and Robert would be putty in her hands. Pity that didn't work with Luke.

Now, thought Roxanne, *it's my turn. While the cat's away* . . . She surveyed the faded velvet curtains and repugnant patterned floor covering. Whoever chose them had no taste whatsoever. She could envisage beautiful gold brocade curtains with a warm beige deep-pile carpet. Next, the chairs needed recovering — she knew Luke wouldn't replace them; and only last week she'd seen some fabulous wallpaper that would look wonderful on the walls . . . She could see it all, and meant to stamp her authority on the whole place. Perhaps if she suggested making the changes on Robert's behalf . . . Obviously Robert was going to find things more and more difficult as his eyesight deteriorated. She would tackle Luke over dinner — strike while the iron was hot, as they said. Lucas would feel wrong-footed by his tardiness.

The door opened and Luke strode in. 'Sorry I'm late,' he murmured, heading for the drinks tray to help himself to a whiskey. 'There just aren't enough hours in the day for what there is to do around here. Have you had a pleasant day, Roxy love? I'm sorry I didn't return for lunch.'

Roxanne rose to her feet and headed in the direction of the dining room without a word. When they were seated, she waved a piece of paper. 'I've had a letter from Jane. She says she's hopeful the eye specialist in America can do something for Robert. If nothing else, he can perhaps slow down the deterioration.'

'Well, that is good news,' Lucas replied, shaking out his napkin. 'I expect it will be a long process, though. I can't see Father being able to do much for quite some time. Not that I mind. He has to do what is best for himself. I can manage things here. Once I streamline things a bit more, it shouldn't be so time-consuming. Besides, at his age it's time he took things easy.'

Mrs Crabbe, anticipating their arrival, began serving the soup, but her manner was decidedly frosty. She despised their lax behaviour. Sir Robert and Lady Victoria would never have behaved in such a manner. As soon as she left the room, Roxanne demanded to know why Mrs Crabbe was still employed by them if she couldn't go about her work in a more pleasant manner.

'She's an institution,' Luke replied, breaking open his bread roll. 'The domestic side of Chellow Hall runs on oiled wheels because of her. Heaven knows how we'd manage if she left; and besides, does it really matter that she's so dour? It's just her nature. We can't all be light-hearted and frivolous like you, my love.'

Light hearted and frivolous, thought Roxanne. *How could one be light-hearted in this draughty, outdated heap of stone?* 'I was looking around; and thinking, while I waited for you, that it's an ideal opportunity while Robert and Jane are away for us to do some refurbishing. We could make things so much easier for Robert. You know, really the whole house could do with a makeover. I would enjoy organising it, and it would give me something to do while you are so occupied.'

'I'm afraid we can't afford it, old girl,' Luke said, finishing his soup just as Mrs Crabbe reappeared. 'Very nice,

Mrs Crabbe.' He still had his mind on the never-ending bills that needed paying. He was determined to show his father he could make a go of running the estate without his help. The last thing he needed right now was another dose of unnecessary expenditure.

'What do you mean, we can't afford it?' Roxanne shrieked as soon as the main course was served. 'I haven't told you of my plans about how we could spruce the place up a bit, or got any estimates yet!'

Luke sighed wearily. 'Well, don't bother, because you'll only be disappointed, I'm afraid. Money doesn't grow on trees, you know. I'm struggling as it is, and now we have to provide for Thomas's future too. How is the little fellow? I really must look into the nursery more often. He seems to have grown every time I see him. He's such a grand little chap, isn't he? I wouldn't be surprised to see him crawling before long.'

Roxanne ground her teeth with

anger. Why did she put up with this travesty of a marriage? It would be different if she had a title. That would have made things slightly more bearable. Why Jane should be addressed as 'Lady' was beyond her; common as muck, she was, and it showed.

'Tomorrow I'm off to London,' Roxanne snapped. Rising to her feet, carelessly knocking over her wine glass, she threw down her napkin, leaving her meal untouched, and glared angrily at her husband. 'I don't know when I'll be back — if ever. Not that you would notice my absence. I'm just another expensive encumbrance, aren't I? Another liability on the balance sheet. Why did you marry me, Lucas? Was it just to beget an heir? Well, I guess in that case I'm redundant, aren't I?' With that, she stomped out of the room, slamming the door and making the chandelier jangle alarmingly.

She did rather hope after her tantrum that Luke would relent and would feel guilty enough to seek her out and make up, but she waited in vain. She spent a restless night, frustrated and annoyed. The next morning, she threw clothes haphazardly into a suitcase, cursing all the while. He probably expected *her* to apologise, like a meek little housewife. Like Jane or Annabel would, no doubt. Well, he should know her better by now. She was leaving, and not before time. She might never come back.

Without a second thought for Thomas, she left. Peppering pebbles like gunshot, Roxanne roared down the drive in the car, narrowly missing the gardener hard at work trimming the shrubbery. He had the cheek to shake his fist at her! If she weren't in such a hurry, she'd stop and fire him on the spot. Just who did he think he was? London beckoned like a homing beacon. Her old stamping ground. The bright lights, the shops and theatres — everything she had given up to become Mrs Lucas Wylde of Chellow Hall. Had it all been a mistake? When they were first married, she had been besotted with Lucas and his connections, but somewhere along the line the shine had gone off their relationship. How she wished she hadn't given up her career so easily. Who knew what she might have achieved if she had remained a model? And yet she had given it all up to please Lucas. Not that he appreciated her sacrifice, apparently.

As she motored down the A1, she mulled over their stormy marriage, and couldn't pinpoint exactly when it had all changed. *What on earth did he expect of me? Didn't he ever wonder what I did all day?* She couldn't spend all and every day riding, and shopping in the likes of York or Leeds was laughable. *Maybe,* she thought with a grimace, *a few days on his own might bring him to his senses.* If not, then they were surely heading for the divorce courts before she got too old to start a new relationship. She didn't relish the prospect, but knew they couldn't go on the way they were doing. She was beginning to regret adopting Thomas. She'd found she had no maternal instincts and wasn't at all bothered about him. Also, he was going to be an added complication if they did separate. There was no way she wanted to be burdened with him.

Arriving in London, she booked into the Savoy, knowing it would annoy Luke — he would view it as an extravagance, but she felt like pampering herself, and to hell with the expense. A good session at the beauty parlour and a few shopping sorties should work wonders. On the way down, she had resolved to pay a visit to her old modelling agency too, and cautiously ask if they could put any jobs her way. It had been seven years since she had last worked, but felt she could still hold her own against the younger models. She was always figure-conscious, and had experience and a standing in the community, which must count for something. If she could get one assignment, it would give her added confidence — something she'd lacked since being relegated to the depths of rural Yorkshire. When she'd first married, Chellow Hall had epitomised all she ever wanted, but now she wasn't so sure. That was one thing she could agree with Jane about. Living at Chellow Hall wasn't all it was cracked up to be.

★   ★   ★

It felt good to be back — back in the civilised world. Three days had elapsed, and now Roxanne approached the model agency feeling polished and sharp. Having spent a fortune at the beauty salon, the hairdressers and numerous chic boutiques, she felt energised and rejuvenated. Seven years was a long time to be out of the modelling scene, but maybe that absence could work in her favour, especially with her aristocratic background. See Freddie, and . . . Would he be perceptive enough to notice the tiny lines skilfully hidden by make-up and the odd extra pound in weight she carried? Only that morning she had gazed critically at herself in the mirror, and knew she was deceiving herself into thinking she looked the same as she had before marriage. Her stomach churned with nervousness, and she wished she'd had more than grapefruit for breakfast. It had been a mistake — she could see that now.

Roxanne sighed. Trying to gloss over the truth was pointless. Like the many phone calls she had made to so-called friends who were not available, or too busy to spare the time to have lunch with her, even. She was feeling lost and lonely and wished Luke would ring to beg her to return, but she was loath to be the first to give in. He was the one at fault. He deserved to be taught a lesson.

Stiffening her shoulders, she marched boldly into the dreary offices. Nothing ventured, nothing gained. Things didn't look too prosperous. No decorating had been done; the reception chairs still looked exactly the same, shabby and uncomfortable. The smell of cooking wafted in from the café next door. No, nothing had changed, so what on earth was she doing there? She was about to walk out, not wanting to waste anyone's time — least of all her own — when the receptionist bobbed up from behind the desk.

'Can I help you?' she asked in a somewhat bored fashion, hardly taking the time to look at Roxanne. The papers she had retrieved were obviously more important.

'I've come to see Freddie. He's still in charge here, I presume?' Roxanne declared imperiously.

The girl looked up and frowned. 'You haven't got an appointment, have you? I'll see if he's available. Who shall I say wants to see him?'

Roxanne bit her tongue, unsure of whether she wanted to go through with her plan. In the past, she'd had a crush on Freddie. He'd given her the break into modelling when other agencies had turned her down. It had been Freddie who had guided her in her first stumbling steps on the career ladder, for which she felt indebted, even though at times he could be brutal to the point of being cruel.

'Just tell him it's Roxanne . . . Roxanne Meadows.'

The girl picked up the phone, but almost immediately the door behind her burst open and Freddie appeared, beaming broadly. Obviously he still spied on his outer office. Roxanne was quite taken aback by the change in him. He seemed to have aged far more than she would have expected. His hair was now totally grey, and he'd put on an appalling amount of weight.

'Roxanne, darling,' he said, putting an arm around her shoulders and leading her obsequiously into his office. 'Wherever did you spring from? It's so wonderful to see you. Looking beautiful as ever. I wish I had more like you on my books. I'd make a fortune. Today they come in flaunting their portfolios and expect me to swoon with delight. They have no idea . . . '

'How are things, Freddie?' Roxanne composed herself on the offered chair and smiled. 'I came down to do a spot of shopping, and thought I would look you up for old times' sake.'

'Well, it's lovely to see you, my dear. Of course, you married well, and went to live in the country, didn't you? Somewhere up north, wasn't it? Lucky you,' he said, eyeing her expensive clothes. 'You look well, so marriage obviously suits you.'

'It has its compensations,' she replied nonchalantly, 'but I do miss the buzz of London. Living in Yorkshire, one feels totally out of touch.'

He nodded understandingly. 'I don't suppose you miss the early-morning starts, the long days, or the cold draughty studios though, do you?' He laughed, then paused. 'You know, if you lived a bit nearer, I could perhaps fix you up with some part-time work occasionally. I've still got a few contacts. How about it?'

Roxanne chuckled, not wanting to appear eager, but desperate to take him up on his offer. 'What sort of work do you think I could get at my age? I've been out of it for several years, you know.'

Freddie leaned back in his chair and gazed at her. 'If I thought you were seriously interested, I'd fix you up with a calendar job. I know a guy who's looking for someone like you. He rang me only this morning, as a matter of fact.' He spread his hands on the desk and grimaced. 'I'm afraid that, since you left, things have gone steadily downhill. I don't get the lucrative jobs anymore like I used to. Maybe I'm just getting too old and cynical. I've been in the business too long.'

Roxanne left after half an hour of reminiscing, feeling sorry for Freddie and for herself. She had a good husband and a home to be proud of, so why did she feel so downcast? What did she want from life? Someone to love her, be with her, value her. Was that asking too much of a husband? She realised the estate didn't run itself, but she believed Lucas didn't delegate enough. She felt the farm managers ought to be able to do more of the work without Luke's supervision, but no he had to keep an eye on what they were doing all the time.

She spent the rest of the day browsing the shops, but didn't find much to interest her, and returned to the Savoy in low spirits. She wasn't looking forward to another evening on her own, and was debating whether to have a meal sent to her room — perhaps even pack and return home . . .

'I believe you dropped this.'

The man holding her scarf was manna from heaven. Dark hair, midnight-black eyes, teasing smile — and if that wasn't enough, his dark grey suit enhanced his obviously remarkable physique. He knew he was eye-catching, and Roxanne immediately controlled her thoughts. Graciously, she took the scarf he proffered.

'Thank you,' she murmured, and would have moved on, but the man didn't step aside as she expected.

'Pardon me for asking, but aren't you that famous film star . . . I forget the name.' He banged his head with his hand. 'I'm sorry. My manners. I shouldn't . . . '

Roxanne smiled with amusement. 'My name is . . . ' She paused, and decided to play along with his little game. 'Roxy. I am a model. Perhaps you've seen my picture on some magazine cover.'

'So,' he replied, 'that must be it. I hope I haven't offended you.'

'Not at all. I'm flattered. Perhaps you'd care to join me for a drink so I can thank you properly for returning my scarf?'

Roxanne sparkled. The man, Dean, was the exact opposite of Lucas. He was attentive, charming, witty, and extremely attractive. He was knowledgeable about the London scene, and over dinner they discussed and cheerfully argued about the famous art galleries and theatres. The evening was a huge success, and she couldn't be sure later how they ended up in her room. She seemed to remember him saying something about getting a taxi. It was late, and she suggested he went up to her room to phone from there.

Another glass of wine, and somehow one thing led to another, and . . . well . . . without it seeming to be a problem, they were planning to spend the next two or three days together. Dean had no commitments until the following weekend.

Roxanne relaxed in the bath, wondering if she had taken leave of her senses. She knew nothing about him — except what he'd told her, and *that* she took with a pinch of salt. But . . . oh, what the hell! She deserved a few days' decadent excitement. Lucas would never know, so no harm done.

After several deliriously happy days and nights in Dean's company, Roxanne returned home, determined not to become a rural cabbage. It was the start of her newfound interest in keep-fit — or that was the excuse she gave Luke for the weekly visit to York. *Escorts Anonymous* had branches in most major towns, apparently. The men were not all like Dean, but they were available, and definitely seductive. She did at times feel guilty, but decided what Luke didn't know couldn't hurt him. Besides, she was easier to live with; so, in a way, it was doing him a favour.

8

Annabel had been at Holly Bush Farm a month. A very long, arduous month it had been, too. She sat at the kitchen table preparing vegetables for Mr Wylde's dinner, reflecting on the peculiar set-up, and marvelling at how someone reputably rich could be so frugal. Her employer, a God-fearing man, frowned on luxuries to such an extent that Annabel wore two layers of clothes in an effort to keep warm. She had been told in no uncertain manner that her employer considered her too young for the job, but Lady Jane had stuck up for her, saying what an honest and willing worker Annabel was.

Annabel wished she hadn't. She wished . . . but what was the point of wishing? She was stuck with the present situation until her memory returned. *Then what?* she often wondered. *Would it be a blessing?* She got up and poked the fire in the range, bringing it to life ready to cook the stew, and reflected on her earlier struggle to master its eccentricities. She had never heard of using black-leading to clean the stove, or peat as a source of fuel for the fires. Thank goodness for books. That was one thing the farmhouse wasn't short of.

She really didn't belong here, she knew that, but until she could remember something, no matter how trivial, here she would have to remain. She wished she had asked more questions and persuaded Iris Peters to talk. She felt certain Iris knew more than she let on; too late now, though. Nobody here in this small village knew anything about her. Lady Jane suggested this should be a fresh start, and she should try to forget she had a past life, but Annabel wasn't happy about that. She wanted to know just who she really was.

She glanced outside, and thought about exploring the immediate area when the weather improved, which gave her something to look forward to. So far, she had only been to the village and back, always at her employer's bidding. He timed her to make sure she didn't dawdle, so she hadn't had time to see much for herself. She hadn't ventured onto the moor, either, as she had been kept far too busy. The moor looked inhospitable — bleak, wild and forbidding — but Annabel felt sure that when the heather grew again and the sun came out it would look oh so different. Her employer was a hard taskmaster, but she was determined one day to have a few hours out there alone. She surely deserved some time off.

Having been instructed on her first day in what was expected of her, Annabel had set to work with a willing determination to prove herself worthy of the job. She had spring-cleaned the house from top to bottom. It had certainly needed it, and she wondered how long Mr Wylde had been on his own. It had been a mammoth task washing sheets, blankets, curtains and everything using the old dolly tub and mangle, but it meant she was too tired at the end of the day to worry about her past. She literally fell into bed completely exhausted. At least she had a roof over her head, and work to do aplenty.

So far, she had yet to see any wages. She was too scared to ask for any, and in any case, there was little to spend money on here. The village shop stocked the normal basics, but for luxury items, the nearest town was ten miles away. A bus ran once a week collecting passengers from all the outlying villages, setting off very early and returning in the late afternoon. Her employer had divulged this information to her in such a manner as to intimate he didn't expect Annabel would be using it. An ancient bicycle was her only mode of transport, then; or else, shank's pony.

Gradually, Annabel was getting to know her way around, and had learned when best to keep out of her employer's way. Life might not be exactly pleasurable, but at least she was not quite destitute, having secreted away the money Lady Jane had given her before she left, keeping it for emergencies. During the past month, she had often contemplated leaving, especially when her employer shouted at her for some minor indiscretion, but anxiety of the world out there — the unknown — frightened her more.

The last time he chastised her — unjustly, she thought — Annabel had walked out of the house, fully determined never to return. It had been about a week ago. He snapped at her, saying the meal was late and uneatable. Annabel felt like throwing it at him, but instead had held her temper and left without a word, head held high. Once clear of the farmhouse, though, she had set off as if demons were after her. She felt so miserable and alone. Why had she no relatives? Where were her parents? Were they dead? She supposed they must be, because otherwise they would have got in touch somehow.

Eventually, she had slowed to amble through the rough bracken, blinking back tears of despair. It was dreadful feeling so alone, with no friends, even. What chance had she of meeting anyone to chat to when her employer kept her so busy? Mr Wylde was a dour individual, hardly ever smiled, and didn't invite any sort of conversation.

Then suddenly, out of nowhere, had appeared Fergus — Fergus Soames. Thinking about him now, Annabel blushed. She'd found him very attractive, but knew she would become tongue-tied in his presence if they were to meet again. She had seen him a couple of times in the distance this past week, accompanied by Nell, his sheep-dog.

Why had she blurted out her strange predicament to him, a complete stranger? For some reason she had unburdened herself then, and he had listened so patiently. In the end, he'd smiled a slow, lazy smile, and told her to follow her heart. If things got too unpleasant, then of course she ought to leave, but Annabel should be aware of the difficulties Percy Wylde had too. *Talk to him, face up to him,* he'd said. *Don't let him berate you unjustly.* Well, Annabel would do as he suggested. The next time Mr Wylde shouted at her, she would shout back — even if it ended with her dismissal. Things couldn't get much worse, could they?

Annabel stirred the stew, resolved to be more positive from now on. Mr Wylde would find things very difficult, if not impossible, without her. Annabel wondered how he had managed before she came, and how many housekeepers he had gone through. Apparently nobody stayed long, and that was no surprise to her. Who had provided the stockpile of logs and peat, for instance? He must have leant heavily on good neighbours, but so far Annabel had yet to meet them. The only person she had met was Fergus, and that was by accident. Perhaps he was their only neighbour?

Her employer informed Annabel at the outset that he used to regularly walk to the village church each Sunday, but had stopped when a new vicar arrived. He didn't take to his newfangled ideas. Annabel surmised that it was because he found the journey too much for him now, especially in bad weather. He also told her about the vegetable plot that needed attention — he didn't expect to have to pay fancy prices for potatoes. That would be another chore to add to her duties.

It was a few weeks later that Annabel learned Fergus was married and had a small son. It came about quite unexpectedly when she met his wife, Fiona, and their child as they were leaving the village shop. Annabel had been despatched to post some letters for her employer, and needed to buy some lard and flour. Fiona introduced herself and their lively five-year-old, Thomas. She was easy-going and friendly, and suggested Annabel might like to drop in to see them whenever her chores permitted. In the end, she waited while Annabel made her purchases, and the two of them walked part way back to the farmhouse together. Fiona told her she'd been a nurse before she married Fergus, and still kept her hand in when emergencies arose. 'So if ever you have a problem, do give me a shout,' she said as they parted company. 'We live just over the hill, about half a mile away.'

That was the beginning of Annabel's nightmares. Every night she was loath to go to sleep. The name Thomas was familiar, but she didn't know why; and always in her dream there was the vision of a small baby with a mat of thick red hair, crying his eyes out because his mother had deserted him. Annabel became convinced she was that mother. That was why she had amnesia — because she had done something so terrible. She must have abandoned her baby. If only she could remember. She would do anything ... anything. Could she ask Fiona? How would she know if she'd had a baby?

Each morning, Annabel awoke feeling exhausted and hardly up to the workload she had to shoulder. She cleaned and dusted, cooked and mended like a robot. She stoked the fires and dug the garden until she was on the verge of collapse. She was so haunted by guilt that she tried to expunge it with work, but to little effect.

9

Roxanne too felt guilty, but it didn't worry her the way it did Annabel. The excursions to York and Harrogate were the highlight of her week. *Escorts Anonymous* were very discreet, and had several suitable locations where clients could meet in private, knowing they wouldn't be disturbed. Roxanne always took the precaution of wearing a wig, and often a large floppy hat and dark glasses, to avoid recognition. She enjoyed the pretence of a cloak-and-dagger experience. Some of the men she met were far too brash and full of themselves, but Wesley was different. It wasn't just because he was foreign. Wesley was beautifully articulate, and a perfect gentleman. The afternoons Roxanne spent in his company were tremendously exciting. Sometimes they just chatted over a glass of wine, but to her it was money well spent as far as she was concerned. For the first time in a long while, she was feeling alive and loved.

Roxanne couldn't see why anything should bring such a perfect arrangement to an end. Luke, exceedingly busy with estate matters, seemed delighted she had found something with which to occupy herself. The proposed refurbishment hadn't been mentioned, and Roxanne was more serene and accommodating. Life was returning to normal . . . until she began to feel off-colour. Every morning she awoke feeling dreadful. She didn't want to get out of bed, and didn't feel like eating anything. Then she began to be sick.

Luke was concerned, and wanted to send for the doctor, but Roxanne wouldn't hear of it. 'It must be something I've eaten,' she declared. 'I'll be right as rain again soon.' But for all her brave words, she was worried. What if she'd caught something — some unmentionable disease? Whatever would Luke say then? She considered every possibility, every likely cause, until eventually she had to accept the obvious answer — she was pregnant. She was having great difficulty in accepting the fact, since she had been told it was most unlikely she would ever be able to conceive. She hadn't given any thought to preventative measures, although most of her escorts had enquired. It was her own fault. She couldn't blame them, much as she would like to. She decided she had to get away and have some time alone to review her options, so she informed Luke she needed to go to London.

'Are you sure you are well enough, my dear?' he said, clearly anxious about her.

She nodded. 'I think I'll go by train, though. I did promise Mary I would attend her wedding anniversary party, so I don't want to let her down. It will probably do me good to have a change of scene for a couple of days.'

'Well, if you're sure . . . I'm afraid I can't take time off at the moment to accompany you. You could get Pettigrew to drive you if you like, I shan't be needing him.'

'No, it's all right, I think I'd prefer to go by train in this instance,' she replied quickly. 'I'm not sure how long I'll be away, you know how Mary can be so demanding. I'll try not to let her bamboozle me into staying too long, though.'

The visit to Harley Street confirmed her worst fears. She was indeed pregnant. Sitting in the train on the way home, she reviewed the enormity of her condition. If she told Lucas she was pregnant, she knew he would be thrilled to bits — but she also knew without a shadow of doubt that the baby wasn't his. It was possible . . . more than likely . . . that the baby could be Wesley's. It could be black, like him. If that were the case, she wouldn't be able to pass it off as Luke's, even with the best of explanations. Whatever was she to do?

She certainly couldn't tell Wesley. He was a married man. He'd made it plain from the start he only got involved because he needed the money. He'd no intention of leaving his wife and family. It was for their benefit he had joined *Escorts Anonymous*, so he could give them a better lifestyle. For the first time in her life, Roxanne began to accept she had been totally irresponsible, and felt petrified about the consequences.

On her return she put on a brave face, pretending she felt much better, but kept out of Luke's way as much as possible, for make-up could only go so far in hiding her pasty countenance. She went to the nursery and stared at Thomas, wondering if she could possibly bring herself to go through with the pregnancy. Would she be more appreciative of her own child? For days, Roxanne couldn't bear to leave the house, fearful that her condition showed and everyone would know her guilty secret. She was glad Jane wasn't around. She would probably have guessed and said how thrilled she was.

One afternoon, Roxanne decided she would have to exercise Demon. She knew Lucas would begin asking questions if she didn't, since he knew how much she loved riding, and she had missed it for nearly three weeks. She had come to the conclusion that the only way was to behave as naturally as possible until she could arrange to have an abortion. That seemed the only possible answer. The thought horrified her, but the alternative was too depressing to contemplate. She had so wanted a child to please Luke when they were first married, and now she was considering getting rid of one, but there seemed to be no alternative. If only she could be sure the baby was white . . .

Demon seemed pleased to see her. She gave him a couple of sugar lumps while the groom saddled him, and then set off with the intention of having a gentle plod round the estate. It did feel good to be out riding again; and the fresh air and exercise, she thought, would do her good.

Once clear of the stable yard, though, Demon had other ideas. With a toss of his head, he went wild with pleasure. Having been cooped up for far too long, he galloped off, taking hedges and ditches with enthusiasm. Roxanne's feeble attempts to rein him in were completely ignored. Not that she minded. Demon was enjoying his freedom and she knew how he felt. It was exhilarating. He galloped faster and faster. *Maybe that's the answer,* she thought, *a miscarriage.* Hadn't she heard somewhere that pregnant women shouldn't ride? Perhaps there would be no need to go to London again after all . . .

So, instead of holding him back, she urged him on. Faster and faster they went, until they entered the woods, and even then Demon hardly slowed.

Roxanne was so wrapped up in her private thoughts that when Demon stopped abruptly she was taken completely by surprise. The horse had been about to leap the river, which normally he would have done easily, but a deer startled him. The upshot was that Roxanne flew gracefully over his head, landing slap in the middle of the water. She had no time to save herself, if indeed she even tried. She just accepted the inevitable. It wouldn't be the first time she had been thrown — but it had never been into a river before. An earlier vision of Annabel flashed through her mind. Was Roxanne now being repaid for all her injustices?

10

Jon and Patsy were having another of their interminable rows. 'For crying out loud, why ever did you marry me, Patsy?' Jon retorted angrily. 'It surely wasn't out of love.'

'That was Father's idea, not mine. I was quite happy being single. I don't need a man to take care of me.'

'Of course, appearance is everything with your father, isn't it? He couldn't stand the thought of his darling daughter not being able to trap a man, so he went looking for one on her behalf. And *I* fitted the bill nicely, didn't I? He liked the idea of being associated with the Wyldes of Chellow Hall. It gives him some standing amongst his so-called friends, and got you off his hands into the bargain.'

Patsy scowled. 'It took care of your IOUs, don't forget. You could have been sent to prison. My father did you a huge favour.'

'Something you'll never let me forget,' Jon snapped. 'I might have been better off in prison than under your thumb.'

'It was explained to you at the outset I would carry on with my career. I do not intend to leave the earning of money to you. Not with your track record.'

Jon stuck his hands in his pockets and wandered over to stare out of the window. 'With the right incentive, I could change.'

'Leopards do not change their spots,' she spat back.

That hit below the belt. He turned to look at her smug, self-righteous face. 'If you were pregnant . . .'

She looked absolutely horrified at the very idea. 'I have no inclination to breed, so you can put that thought right out of your head,' she said with an irritable toss of the head. 'At least not for the foreseeable future.'

'But since Luke and Roxy haven't so far produced an heir, Father is relying on me. He needs a son to inherit Chellow.'

'Tough, because it won't be with me, at least not yet a while. Time for that when I've made my fortune. I fully intend on showing my father just how clever I can be. I won't own just one hotel, but a whole damned chain of them before I'm very much older. I'll show him I'm as good as any son he might have had.'

'Don't you mean *we*?'

Patsy smirked. 'You forget, the business is in my name, and that's the way it's going to stay. It was my father's wedding present to me. I shall continue giving you pocket money, providing you do your bit to earn it.'

Jon growled and looked about to slap her, but thought better of it. Without her, he would be penniless, so until he could save enough to be self-sufficient he would have to put up with his farcical marriage. His father would show him no mercy, and he couldn't expect Luke to do anything to help either. This time he would have to do it himself, once he'd got a stake. He vowed that this time, though, he'd not do it at the gambling tables. He'd learned his lesson the hard way. 'One of these days . . . just don't push me too far, Patsy, or I won't be responsible for my actions.'

Patsy gave a coarse laugh. 'I know you too well, my love. You will never be anything but a stupid fool. I only married you for your name. As Mrs Patsy Wylde, I have a much better chance of being taken seriously business-wise. Now, be a good boy and see the guests are being attended to. That is what I pay you for, and if you do a good job I may even give you a pay rise. I've got work to do planning where I'll open up my next hotel.'

Jon stormed out. One way or another, before he was very much older, he was going to earn some money and be free of her for good. She could have her precious chain of hotels, but he wanted nothing to do with it. He had plans of his own.

Meanwhile, Patsy had ideas buzzing round her head. She had put out feelers for another property which she could buy cheaply and do up. The prospect pleased her enormously and she perused papers avidly for any worthwhile hotel — or property she could turn into one. She particularly fancied being back in England again, especially London. That would give her the reputation she was seeking and show her father he didn't need a son as an heir. It still annoyed her that women were not taken seriously in the marketplace, but perhaps in the future — who knew?

11

Roxanne awoke feeling confused and light-headed. Why was she in bed when it was broad daylight? Gradually, she recollected that she had been out with Demon, and he had come to a shuddering stop. She recalled being thrown head-first into the river. She remembered vividly the water closing over her head — how terrifying it was!

She shuffled in bed to make herself more comfortable. Obviously, she hadn't died and gone to heaven, that much was quite apparent. Looking around, she recognised her own bedroom, and she was wearing one of her prettiest nightgowns. She stretched awkwardly and realised she ached all over. Then there were questions to be answered. How had she got here? Who had found her? Who saved her? She was about to ring the bell when the door opened and Lucas hesitantly poked his head round.

'Come in, Luke,' she croaked.

'Ah, good. You're awake. How are you feeling?' Luke approached the bed, looking worried.

'I'm fine, never better,' she replied tersely. 'How did I . . . ? Who . . . ?'

Lucas sat on the edge of the bed, smiled lovingly, and took hold of her hand. 'You were extremely lucky, my darling. One of the estate workers some distance away saw what happened, so managed to drag you out of the river before running for help. His quick thinking saved your life. Let's hope you haven't got pneumonia. I'm just about to send for the doctor.'

Roxanne shivered. 'Don't bother with a doctor. I'm fine, honestly. I don't know what got into Demon. Is he all right? He didn't come to any harm, did he?'

Lucas laughed. 'Trust you to be more interested in the damned horse's well-being! Yes, he's none the worse for his experience, although for what he did to you I think he should be shot. You were lucky not to be killed.'

'It wasn't his fault. Truly, it wasn't. I had my mind on other things and let him have his head. And really, I don't need a doctor, I'm fine. I'll get up soon. I'm so sorry to have caused an upset.'

'Are you sure, Roxanne? You've not been yourself lately. Wouldn't it be better . . . ?'

'Yes. I'm positive. I don't want mollycoddling.' She sounded snappish, but then relented and softened it with a smile. 'Truly, I don't want to be a nuisance. I really am fine.'

'How about I get Mrs Crabbe to bring you something to eat now; then if you feel like getting up later, we can have dinner together quietly?'

Roxanne nodded her agreement. 'Something light — an omelette, maybe.'

Left alone, Roxanne reflected on her predicament. She supposed she was still pregnant and the accident hadn't produced a miscarriage, more was the pity. Somehow, she would have to get herself to a London clinic she knew of, without Luke discovering her guilty secret. Thank goodness he hadn't called the doctor. The old family doctor would surely have informed Luke of her pregnancy. The sooner she had the abortion the better, so she had better start eating to show him she was fit and well.

She spent the next week lazing around, taking things easy, but was increasingly desperate to get to London. Eventually, she decided she was fit enough to drive. She still felt weak and anxious about what she intended doing, but knew there was truly no other course open to her. She informed Lucas she wanted to see a specialist to see if they could recommend a course of treatment that would help her get back her stamina. She said she hated being so lethargic. He was delighted, and even offered to drive her, but she managed to persuade him not to, saying she was better going on her own as she might take the opportunity to hit the shops while she was there. He didn't take much persuading after that, because he was extremely busy, but promised they would have a holiday when she returned. Roxanne rang the Harley Street private clinic, and fortunately managed to get an early appointment.

She wasn't in a hurry this time as she headed south. She drove sedately since she had a lot on her mind, bitterly regretting the way she had behaved recently. She felt sorry for letting Lucas down, and made a promise to herself that she would make a determined effort to be a better person in future. She would try harder to be the sort of wife expected of her, and prayed she could have another child, fathered by Lucas — although perhaps maybe Lucas couldn't father children. She had thought all along it was her fault they were barren. Oh dear, poor Luke — and she couldn't even tell him.

She was determined to make a fresh start when she returned by taking more of an interest in Thomas. Surely it couldn't be so difficult. Didn't everyone feel more maternal with their own offspring? She began thinking of the toys she could bring back for Thomas and Sophie. It might be quite fun to shop for the children . . .

The weather was perfect. The sun shone from a clear blue sky — dazzlingly so. Roxanne hummed to herself as she motored south, trying to hide how desperate she felt. If all went well, she could be home by the weekend. She wondered what Dean or Wesley would say if they knew about the baby. Would they be horrified at what she was planning to do? But there really was no alternative.

An hour into her journey, with the sun in her eyes making her head ache, she was considering stopping for a coffee break when she first saw the smoke. She wondered if someone had lit a bonfire, or had there been an accident. As she crested a slight rise, she noticed the vehicles in front slowing down. She followed suit, hoping they wouldn't be delayed for long, and wishing she had stopped at the last village. She pulled in to the side of the road and stopped, tapping her fingers irritably on the steering wheel. The next thing she saw in the rear-view mirror was a heavy lorry bearing down on her, and it wasn't stopping. She stared, mesmerised, knowing there was nothing she could do. It just kept coming and coming. Eventually, she screamed and screamed.

★ ★ ★

It was several hours later that Lucas received the news. His wife was dead. The car was a mangled heap of scrap, and Roxanne had died instantly.

12

'I shall be away for the next day or two,' Annabel's employer growled late one morning, 'and I don't expect you to take advantage of my absence to skive. There's still plenty for you to do, especially in the garden. Make sure it's well-watered if the dry weather continues.'

'Yes, of course,' Annabel replied, trying to hide her pleasure on hearing the news. She had been wondering what was going on ever since the telegram boy had come. She thought immediately it was bad news, but since it meant Mr Wylde was going away, it was good news for her at least.

'Pettigrew will be here this afternoon; so don't just stand there, girl, go and fetch my suitcases out of the attic, there's packing to be done. I hope my shirts are clean, and I need my dark suit. See that the trousers are pressed and my shoes are polished. And find my black tie.'

So, whatever had happened, it concerned Chellow Hall, mused Annabel as she did her employer's bidding. As far as she could recall, telegram boys only ever delivered bad news of people dying. She wondered who had died. She didn't dare ask as her employer was in one of his domineering moods. She was chivvied for the rest of the morning, and was mightily relieved to see Pettigrew when he arrived earlier than expected.

'Don't waste time, girl,' Mr Wylde snapped when Annabel thoughtfully waited by the gate to wave him off. 'Go and get the cleaning done, and change the sheets on my bed.'

As soon as the car disappeared from sight, Annabel breathed a huge sigh of relief and instantly decided, no matter what he had told her, that it was an ideal opportunity for her to go for a walk. The housework could wait. The sun was out, and as far as she was concerned, she was free to do as she pleased for a couple of days. She fully intended making the most of the time on her own. She felt she deserved a few hours to do just as she wanted, and knew exactly what first. She would go and see Fiona. The pleasant woman had told her many a time to call in, but Annabel hadn't felt able to take her up on the invitation so far. This would be the best opportunity she would ever have.

After damping down the fire she hurriedly locked up and set off, walking at a brisk pace across the heather. Finding a narrow track — made by the sheep, she supposed — she wandered happily, enjoying the peace and tranquillity. The wind was cool and clouds occasionally obscured the sun, but she didn't care. It was wonderful being out there, free as a bird. She had no difficulty in finding the farmhouse, and only as she opened the gate did she pause to wonder if now would be convenient.

Fiona appeared at the door and waved. She said she was delighted to see Annabel and immediately set about making a pot of tea and buttering some freshly-baked scones. 'You've escaped,' she said, her eyes twinkling merrily. 'How did you manage it? I wondered if you would ever make it over here. Mr Wylde's a proper slave-driver.'

'He was called away,' Annabel replied, beaming with delight. 'So I thought I would take myself off for a walk — before, of course, I get on with all the whole heap of chores he has told me to do.'

Fiona pulled a face. 'I'm glad you came. We don't get many visitors, so it's nice to have someone to talk to. How long will he be gone?'

Annabel shrugged her shoulders. 'He didn't say. A day or two, maybe. I think it's a funeral he's attending.'

'Oh dear. Will you be all right on your own?' Fiona said thoughtfully. 'Yon place is rather isolated. I'm not sure I would feel comfortable here on my own.'

'Oh yes, I'll be grand,' Annabel replied and quickly changed the subject. She wasn't entirely happy about being alone in the house, but what else could she say? 'Where's Thomas?'

Fiona glanced out of the window. 'He's with his dad in the barn. They'll both be back any minute, I should imagine. They can smell my baking a mile away.'

Almost immediately they heard the back door open, and in rushed Fiona's son, followed more leisurely by Fergus. Annabel was delighted to see them. They made her most welcome. The next hour was exceedingly pleasant, chatting to Fiona and Fergus, and Annabel started to relax. It had been such a long time since she had felt happy. She couldn't remember the last time she had actually laughed. How long had she been at Holly Bush Farm — three months? It seemed like years.

She smiled at Thomas playing with a kitten.

'Don't do that,' Fiona told him, as he seemed intent on teasing the poor little thing to death.

Thomas took no notice. Eventually, as predicted, the kitten unsheathed its claws and lashed out. Thomas cried out in alarm.

'Oh, Tommy, what did I tell you?' his mother said. 'Has it scratched you?' She quickly scooped the child up, and examined his hand. 'Back in a moment,' she said to Annabel as she carried him off to the bathroom to find some antiseptic.

Annabel nodded, but hardly took in what Fiona had said — she was stunned by the name she had called her son. Tommy. *Tommy*. Where had she heard that name before? Images flashed before her eyes: images of a small baby. It was like being hit by a shaft of lightning.

Annabel leapt out of the chair and hurriedly shouted her goodbyes. Fergus — who had rescued the kitten and was issuing it into a box by the Aga — called after her, saying he would see she got back all right, but she would have none of it.

'No. No. It's all right!' she shouted. 'I prefer to be on my own. Thanks for everything.' And she rushed off, not caring if she appeared rude. She wanted — *needed* — to be alone, to think. *Thomas, Tom, Tommy.* What was it? Was her father called Thomas? Yes, that was it, her father was called Thomas — Thomas Masters, but more often called Tommy, and she named her baby after him . . .

She slowed when she suddenly had a vision of an old-fashioned pram with a tiny baby in it — her baby. He was called Tommy. Not Tom or Thomas, just Tommy.

She next had a clear recollection of Roxanne's horse clipping her and sending her over the bridge into the icy water. Everything was coming back to her. She had been home for Christmas and had given birth to her son. She was on her way back to Chellow Hall to confront his father — or, more likely Jon's father, Sir Robert. At least, she had started out to do just that, but had changed her mind. Jon was recently married, and she had perhaps wondered if he wouldn't believe her story.

But why had they taken her baby away from her? Why? *Why?* What had she done to deserve that, apart from having amnesia? One thing was certain: she meant to find out where her son was. She would find Tommy if it was the last thing she did. They had no right to take him from her. Where could he be? She was almost beside herself with anger and frustration. The Wyldes had a lot to answer for, by Jove, and she was certain that this time she wasn't going to be thwarted.

Gradually, she calmed down and tried to think more rationally. How was she to get to Chellow Hall? It would be there she needed to start her investigation. The last time she recalled seeing Tommy was by the bridge, so Mrs

Roxanne Wylde was the person she needed to confront. She had always been a troublemaker. Always blaming others for her own mistakes. Although maybe it would be better to see Lady Jane — she would be more approachable.

Annabel vowed to catch the weekly bus first thing in the morning. She had never been on it, but felt sure it would help her get back to Chellow Hall somehow. Anyway, there was nobody to stop her. Hang the housework and the job. Nothing mattered but finding her son. She would demand to know what they had done with Tommy, and she would claim him back from whoever had him. He was her baby. She did wonder if Lady Jane would help, since she had said she was to contact her in an emergency. Well, this was an emergency, but it was too late to write — she needed action before her courage failed her.

Annabel had a restless night and hardly slept a wink. She was up early, eager to be on her way, and was too upset up to eat much, but made a sandwich to have later. With her few possessions, she set off on her journey to Chellow Hall. She arrived at the bus stop in plenty of time; not wanting to speak to her fellow passengers, she went to sit on a large stone a short distance away.

Fortunately, once on the bus, Annabel had a seat to herself, and plenty of time to think as they meandered through the country lanes, stopping at all the moorland villages. Her memory was coming back in dribs and drabs. Her parents had died in the Blitz and the Palmers had taken her in. They had looked after her exceedingly well, and treated her like their very own daughter. When she left school she had worked at the local library. She had always liked books, and enjoyed her work. On her twenty-first birthday, she had discovered she might have relatives still alive and living in Scarborough, so at the first opportunity had taken time off work to see if she could find them.

It was on her trip to Scarborough she had met Jon Wylde. She had been walking along the seafront and had nearly been run down by Jon's sports car. He had apologised most profusely and taken her to a nearby café for coffee, saying it was the least he could do. He certainly had a way about him, and she found herself explaining why she was in Scarborough. She'd had no luck locating her relatives, and was feeling a little down in the dumps. He made her laugh and cheered her up no end. When he learned she was a librarian, he instantly suggested she could work for his father. He was most persuasive, and eventually — goodness knew how he managed it — she agreed to join the staff at Chellow Hall. She had been attracted to Jon, he was so charming and courteous, but she soon realised he was a fickle woman-chaser and not to be trusted. She remembered beginning to catalogue the library at Chellow Hall, and occasionally taking care of Sophie, the three-year-old daughter of Sir Robert and Lady Jane. It seemed like aeons ago.

Then, last autumn, there was a 'flu epidemic; many of the staff were affected, and Lady Jane was concerned when Annabel started with a cold. She immediately sent her to the doctor, which was when she discovered she was pregnant. My, what a shock that had been! She supposed she should have contacted Jon straight away, but he was away on his honeymoon, so it was hardly an appropriate time to inform him he was to be a father. Instead, she had hurried south to the Palmers. They had been simply wonderful. She must get in touch with them as soon as possible; they would be worried sick as she hadn't written to them.

It was late afternoon by the time Annabel arrived at the Hall. The bus had taken forever, stopping at every village on route, with lots of passengers getting off and on. When she reached Whitby, she had stopped on the seafront to have her sandwich before setting off for Chellow Hall. But now she was here, she was unsure of how to go about her intended confrontation. For a start, she didn't know which members of the family would be in residence. Lady Jane had said something about her and Sir Robert and Sophie going to live in Spain for a while. That was three months ago, so maybe they would be back again by now. She didn't know where Jon Wylde was, now he was married — presumably not living at the Hall, though, so she was hardly likely to bump into him.

Suddenly, she had an inspiration. She was approaching the bridge where the accident happened, and she remembered Iris Peters helping her. She would go and see her, and perhaps she could stay the night and learn more about the happenings at the Hall since she left. She felt it would be best to face the onslaught after a good night's sleep — if that was possible — and not now, when she was so desperately tired.

Iris Peters was cautiously surprised to see Annabel on her doorstep. She often wondered what had happened to her. 'You look all in,' she said guardedly. 'Come along, and I'll make some tea.'

'I've come to ask a favour,' Annabel said, once they were sitting in the tidy kitchen with tea and home-made biscuits.

'Oh?'

'I'd like to ask what you know about my accident.'

Iris Peters said nothing; merely frowned and fiddled with the teapot cosy. She would have liked to help the young woman, but didn't want to do or say anything to jeopardise her job.

'The thing is,' Annabel went on with some determination, 'I believe . . . I'm sure I had my son — Tommy — with me, and I must find him. Do you know what happened to him? I'm going out of my mind worrying.'

Iris's hands shook. 'You've come

147

back at a bad time. The funeral's tomorrow. Everything's in chaos.'

'Whose funeral?' Annabel recalled the telegram's arrival, and her guess that there had been a death in the family.

Iris Peters frowned. 'Why, Mrs Roxanne Wylde, that's who. Didn't you know? I guessed that was why you were here.'

Annabel shook her head. 'No, I had no idea. My employer, Mr Percy Wylde, never said. What happened?'

'Car crash.'

Annabel sighed. 'Oh dear, how dreadful.' She paused. 'What am I to do now? What can I do? Someone must know where Tommy is. I must find him.'

Iris Peters chewed her lip. She didn't want to get involved again. It wasn't her responsibility to explain. She'd told them at the time, but would they listen? Lady Jane would have to sort it out.

'You'd best stay here tonight. You can sleep on the sofa. Are they expecting you at the Hall? Most of the rooms are taken, I believe. Some of the relatives have been sent into Whitby. Everything's at sixes and sevens.'

Annabel shook her head. 'Oh, no. Nobody knows where I am. The thing is, my memory suddenly clicked into place. I heard someone call their son Tommy, and it all came back to me. I used to work for Sir Robert, didn't I? And I remember having a sort of accident on the bridge. Demon knocked me into the water, didn't he?'

'Yes, that's right, or so I'm told. About four or five months ago.'

Annabel took a deep breath before continuing. 'The thing is, I know I had my son with me. I'm certain of it. He was in a pram just clear of the bridge. Whatever happened to him? You must know, surely.'

'I'm not sure I should be the one to say,' Iris said slowly.

'But you do know, don't you? I'm not imagining things. My son will be six months old now. I must find him. He's all I've got in the whole wide world.' Then she burst out crying. 'I want my son!'

Iris put a comforting arm round her shoulders. 'There, now, don't take on so. I'm sure everything will be all right. It's just that I don't think it's my place to say what happened.'

'So who will?' Annabel sobbed. 'Tommy is all I have.'

'Perhaps after the funeral you should speak to Lady Jane. Yes, I really do think that would be best. Now, don't you worry.'

Annabel was terribly disappointed, but knew she would learn nothing more from Chellow's most trusted employee. She would just have to wait a little while longer. In any case, she was so tired, she didn't feel she could do much more that day. She certainly wasn't up to facing the Wyldes.

'You stay here tonight,' Iris said. 'Tomorrow's another day. I'm sure everything will work out all right in the end. Now, I must get a move on. I'm on duty this evening.'

Annabel wasn't sure if she should attend the funeral. She would hate Mr Percy Wylde to see her and cause a scene by demanding to know why she wasn't at Holly Bush Farm. Not that she ever intended going back there, but she didn't like confrontations. It was going to be enough of an ordeal speaking to Lady Jane, but she knew it must be done. The sooner, the better; but she realised Lady Jane would be very busy, so it would be difficult finding a time when she was alone.

Annabel watched the funeral proceedings from a safe distance. She felt sorry for Mr Lucas and wished to pay her respects, but didn't feel able to approach him. Sir Robert, she thought, was looking extremely fragile; and Lady Jane seemed — not surprisingly — somewhat harassed. She was surprised to see Jon there — alone. Why hadn't his wife come? Surely a funeral was a time for support from everyone. Sir Robert seemed to be relying on Lady

Jane a lot more, so perhaps his eyesight wasn't improving as they had hoped. She sighed, realising she had come at an awkward moment, but she really did have to talk to Lady Jane and find out what happened to Tommy.

Two days later, after several abortive attempts to see Lady Jane and get into the nursery, she finally managed to sneak up the back stairs unnoticed.

'Annabel? It is you, isn't it? I thought I saw you, but wasn't sure. What are you doing here? I didn't know you were back.'

Annabel snatched her hand from the doorknob and said the first thing that came into her head. 'I've come for my son.' She hadn't meant to sound so cold and accusing, but she had been taken by surprise, so blurted out her intention without a second thought.

Lady Jane gasped. 'Oh. Oh, deary me. How . . . ? Who . . . ?' She looked shell-shocked.

Annabel slumped down on a nearby window seat, afraid her legs might buckle, but determined to follow through with her quest. This was her chance to learn the truth, so it was now or never. 'I heard someone call their son Tommy,' she said quietly, 'and suddenly I remembered — everything. At first I thought it was a dream, but then it was if a cloud lifted, and I recalled falling over the bridge when Mrs Roxanne's horse hit me. Much of what happened after that, and why I was sent to Holly Bush Farm — leaving my son here — is unclear.'

'I see,' Lady Jane said, looking out of the window as if seeking inspiration. 'As you know, things are rather upset around here at the moment. I don't know if I'm on my head or my heels. It will be very useful having you back here again.'

'But you know where my Tommy is, don't you?' Annabel persisted. 'I must see him.'

'Yes, my dear, I quite understand. He's quite safe and well looked-after.'

Annabel shuffled on the edge of the

seat, relieved to have it confirmed at last that she wasn't hallucinating. She really did have a son. 'Why?' she whispered.

'It's rather a long, sad story; but let me say first of all that it was done with the very best of intentions, I assure you. We had no idea at first who the baby belonged to — who the father was. Naturally, we assumed you were his mother; but when you had your accident, you lost your memory. We didn't know what to do. I had the impression you had no relatives we could contact, that you were an orphan. Well, you may remember Roxanne and her husband couldn't have children, so they decided to adopt your child and bring it up as their own. After all, we anticipated you would have great difficulty raising the child on your own, even if you regained your memory. Roxanne believed she was doing you a favour — she truly had your best interests at heart.'

'Roxanne . . . so Tommy *is* here.' She

didn't believe a word of it. Roxanne Wylde would never have done anything that wasn't in her own interests. She was selfish to the last bone in her body, so why had she done it? Unfortunately, Annabel would never know now. 'He's here in the nursery?' She looked about her eagerly. 'I must see him. How could they adopt Tommy without getting my permission? I would never give my child away. Never. It was a dreadful thing to do. Tommy is all I've got.'

Lady Jane put her hand on Annabel's arm. 'No, of course you wouldn't — under normal circumstances. I realise that, Annabel..But these were far from normal circumstances, weren't they? We didn't know if you would ever regain your memory. I couldn't take on the responsibility of looking after another child at the time since Robert was so poorly. I am truly sorry, my dear. We did what we thought was for the best.'

Annabel nodded slowly, not questioning why they hadn't made contact with the Palmers. She had the horrible thought that if Lucas Wylde thought the child was his, then she would have an extremely difficult time getting him back. 'What can I do? I want my child. He's all I have,' she wailed.

Lady Jane smiled sympathetically, patting her hand. 'Shall I make a suggestion? Why don't you come back and work here as nanny to both Thomas and Sophie? It would be a temporary measure until we can think of an alternative. Thomas needs someone anyway, as the last nanny has just left; and of course, now Robert and I are home for a while, I could do with someone to help me with Sophie. When things settle down again, then we'll decide what to do. Lucas has enough on his plate coming to terms with his wife's death without being further upset with your news, don't you think?'

'I suppose so,' Annabel said reluctantly. 'Please, can I see Tommy now?'

'Yes, of course. By the way, we call him Thomas. I hope you don't mind?

Being a Wylde, it sounded better, we thought.'

Annabel nodded in agreement: they were probably right. The Palmers had said as much to her. She couldn't wait to see her son — Tommy, Thomas, whatever.

Together they entered the nursery. There were tears in her eyes when she saw him. He was gorgeous, with lovely red hair and a cheeky grin. She picked him up and vowed never ever to be separated from him again. She would do whatever it took to look after him. Nobody was going to take him away from her care. They might be nobility; they might have lots of money . . . but she was Tommy's mother, and he needed to be with her.

13

It was strange being back at Chellow Hall, but Annabel soon settled in and enjoyed looking after Thomas and Sophie. It was such a relief to be away from Holly Bush Farm, and her new situation gave her time to think and plan what her next step should be. She didn't want to do anything precipitously, since she realised that what Lady Jane had said was true. She would find it very difficult bringing up Tommy — Thomas — on her own when she had no job and nowhere to live. For the last few months at Chellow Hall, he had been well looked-after — wanted. Obviously, this was far better than she would have been able to do on her own . . . but was that sufficient? He was her son, and she wanted desperately to be able to give him a happy upbringing. What should she do? *Give it time*, she thought. *Do nothing in a hurry, especially as it's all the Wyldes' fault in the first place.*

She kept out of the way of all the Wyldes as much as possible, and certainly hoped not to be seen by Percy. She dreaded meeting him again. Lady Jane had said to leave Percy to her, and she would deal with him, but Annabel feared there would be ructions. She definitely wasn't going back to the farmhouse — of that, she was quite certain.

Annabel was alone in the nursery, singing Thomas a lullaby. For the moment, she was quietly content with her situation. She had her son, and she was being paid to look after him. What the future held, only time would tell. Truth be known, she was quite happy.

'Hello. It's Annabel, isn't it? I heard you were back.'

She spun round, clutching Thomas. She hadn't heard the door opening and was speechless to find Lucas Wylde approaching.

'I came to see my son,' he said, looking a little weary but still managing a smile for Thomas. 'I used to try to spend half an hour with him before his bedtime as often as possible. Just lately, though, I've missed the little fellow.'

Annabel didn't know what to say, so held out Thomas, and was stunned to see how eager and happy he was to be cuddled by Lucas. He behaved like he really was Thomas's father.

'Are you happy to be back working here, Annabel?' Luke asked, going to sit on the window seat so he could hold Thomas better.

'Oh yes,' she replied, fearful he was going to suggest she return to Holly Bush Farm.

'Did you manage to sort out your problems at home satisfactorily?'

She frowned, but then recalled her extended Christmas holiday excuse. 'Yes, thank you. Everything's fine at home now.' She began putting toys away and tidying the nursery, feeling nervous in Lucas's presence.

'Will you be able to complete the cataloguing of the library sometime soon, do you think? I know you have Thomas and Sophie to look after, which is quite onerous, but my father is itching to have the library finished.'

'I think . . . if you don't mind me taking To — Thomas — in with me, I could do both at the same time. There isn't a lot more to do. Lady Jane often has Sophie in the mornings, so that would be the best time.'

'Splendid. Better be soon, though, as I suspect this young monkey will soon be crawling all over the place, then you won't have such a free hand.'

Annabel laughed.

★ ★ ★

Over the next few weeks Annabel settled into a calm, orderly regime, looking after Thomas and completing the library work, both responsibilities she enjoyed immensely. She got used to Lucas dropping in to have time with

Thomas, and to Lady Jane, who was friendly and helpful. She didn't see much of Sir Robert or any other members of the family, thankfully. She heard from Lady Jane they had coerced Percy Wylde to remain at Chellow Hall for the time being, which rather dismayed Annabel, so she made a determined effort to stay out of his way. On the few occasions they did meet, he appeared not to recognise her, thank goodness.

Just when Annabel was beginning to feel more confident in her position in the household, one morning she was summoned by a maid to report to Lucas in his study. *What have I done?* she thought anxiously. She couldn't bring to mind anything he could be upset about; so, leaving Tommy with the maid, she approached Luke's study full of trepidation. She desperately hoped she wasn't going to be sent back to Holly Bush Farm. Not that she would go. She would rather go back to London with Thomas than contemplate that again. She tapped on the door.

'Ah, Annabel. Do come in. I want to show you something.' Luke had a newspaper spread out on his desk, and didn't sound at all annoyed. He pointed to a small paragraph halfway down the page. 'Your name is Annabel Masters, isn't it? And you did live in London before you were employed here. So I wondered if this referred to you.'

Annabel quickly scanned the paragraph with growing consternation. 'What does it mean?' she asked. 'Why would some solicitor want to contact me?'

'That's something you ought to find out,' he said with a knowing smile. 'It's probably some sort of inheritance that has been bequeathed to you.'

'Oh no,' she whispered, fearful of some dreadful deed that she couldn't remember. She went quite white and hurriedly sat down.

'Are you all right, my dear?' he asked. 'I didn't mean to upset you. I thought you would be delighted. It should be good news. If you like, I'll make enquiries on your behalf, and let you know if it's anything you should deal with. Will that be all right?'

'Yes, yes . . . thank you, sir. I'd be very much obliged if you would do that. I'm sorry if I'm a nuisance . . . '

'Not at all. I appreciate that the thought of approaching solicitors can be a little daunting for someone like you. As it happens, I'm going into Scarborough this afternoon, so I'll call in and see what I can find out. You leave it with me.'

Annabel smiled her thanks and hurried to the nursery. She cuddled Thomas, dreading that something might happen to take him from her. What was the inheritance likely to be? Would it be enough to help her find a place to live with her son? There was still the problem of Lucas, though — he thought of Thomas as his son, and she didn't think he would easily give him up.

Later that evening, Lucas came to see

her in the nursery. 'You, my dear, *have* been mentioned in someone's will, just as I suspected. I'm not sure how much it is — they wouldn't tell me — but I certainly think you should follow it up.'

'Will? But I don't know anyone,' she murmured, still terrified of something untoward.

'I understand it was a relative you had in Scarborough who has died, and you are to inherit. The solicitors have been trying to trace you for some time. I believe you are the only beneficiary. You shouldn't be scared. You should be pleased. I know it can be bewildering for you, but we'll go to see the solicitor together, if you like? Mr Kemp is known to me.'

'Oh, thank you, sir. I'd be most grateful.'

'That's all right, Annabel. But haven't I told you? None of this *sir* business, and call me Luke. Now, where's my son? Where's my little Thomas?'

* * *

A few days later, Annabel sat in the back of the car, nervously twiddling her thumbs. Luke sat in the front with Pettigrew and began discussing the motor. They were on their way to visit the solicitor in Scarborough, and all Annabel could think about was that she wished she were back in London with the Palmers, before her life had become so topsy-turvy. She was both excited and nervous at the same time. She wasn't sure what to expect, and was glad Lucas would be there to do all the talking. Actually, she thought Lucas sounded more excited than she did.

Pettigrew set them down outside the prestigious offices of Smythe, Trubshaw and Kemp. Annabel gazed in wonderment at the brass plate and marble-floored entrance hall. She would never have dared enter such a place without Lucas urging her on.

'You look as if you are to face a fate worse than death, Annabel,' he said, taking her arm and leading her through the reception area. 'Come, it will soon be over,' he added with a chuckle.

They were not detained long. Mr Kemp, the solicitor, greeted them and settled them in his office with due deference. Annabel sat on the edge of the seat, wide-eyed with anxiety.

'Thank you for coming,' Mr Kemp said, shuffling the papers on his desk. He was an elderly, bespectacled gentleman with a mop of untidy grey hair. He pounced on a bundle of papers and peered over his spectacles at Annabel. 'I would like to get this estate wrapped up as quickly as possible as I am about to retire. It will be easier if I deal with it rather than hand it on to my successor. Miss Broom and her family have been clients of mine for a good number of years. Miss Broom had no close relatives, apparently, but I'll let you have all the details later. To begin with, I'll set your mind at rest and say you will be a wealthy young lady, Miss Masters. The deceased was a Miss Agnes Broom, who I understand was a distant cousin of your mother.'

Annabel sighed. 'Aunt Agnes, of course. I remember her. I came here trying to find her, but got involved in an accident, and . . .'

'Quite so,' Mr Kemp remarked.

Half an hour later, Annabel was being ushered into the car and whisked back to Chellow Hall, dazed by the news — she was an heiress. Dear old Aunt Agnes had left her everything. She wasn't sure what it amounted to. She had been too overwhelmed to hear all that Mr Kemp had told her. Suffice it to say, she would have no more money worries. She would have her own fully-furnished home and money in the bank.

'I will be sorry to see you go,' Lucas said as they walked from the car.

'Go?' she said, puzzled. 'Go where?' Had she missed something?

'Well, I thought that now you have a substantial fortune, you would have no wish to continue working here, for a start. You'll have no need to ever work again, young lady.'

'Oh,' she cried, 'I wouldn't know what to do with myself! I would hate to leave here, and I love looking after Thomas . . . and Sophie. I wouldn't want to go anywhere else.'

He patted her hand. 'I'm so pleased you wish to stay — for the time being, at least,' Luke replied with a grateful smile. 'I expect your good fortune will take some getting used to. When it's all settled, you may feel differently. Do let me know if I can help at any time.'

14

Christmas was approaching, and Annabel reflected on what a difference a year made. Last year, she had been at her wits' end wondering how she was going to cope, and now she had more money than she knew what to do with. It was quite a responsibility. Her life had changed immeasurably. Money obviously mattered more than she had realised, since now at Chellow Hall she was treated more as an equal than as a servant.

Since she had come into her inheritance, so much had changed. For a start, Luke had insisted she join him and the family at mealtimes, and said she was to think of Chellow Hall as her home until she decided where her future lay. He seemed genuinely concerned for her welfare, and Annabel had the sneaking suspicion he was even contemplating asking her to marry him once his mourning period was over. He mentioned more than once that Thomas needed a mother, and how good she was with the child. She liked Luke, and they seemed to get along fine, but she had worries enough with what to do about the house she had inherited, and wasn't at all interested in having her life further complicated with a man problem.

In any case, in more recent times Luke had unobtrusively been keeping company with a certain lady who would probably make a more suitable wife for him. Annabel wasn't in any hurry for matrimony. All she wanted was to live quietly with her son — alone. Unfortunately, the longer Lucas remained in ignorance that Thomas was her son, the more difficult it seemed to find a way of telling him. He had been so kind and helpful that she dreaded upsetting him in any way.

Shortly before Christmas, Annabel set off for Scarborough, having agreed to leave Thomas with Lucas and Rosie, the new nanny Luke had hired. To begin with, Annabel had been hurt at being usurped; but gradually accepted that Rosie was very good with the children, and it did give her some time to herself. Much as she loved her darling son, she felt she needed time to sort out her life quietly on her own. Her mind was in such a whirl with so many things to decide upon.

Her biggest problem was making Seacrest House habitable. By mid-morning, she was walking up the path to it. Her house. Her home. It was a lovely day, sunny but cold, and she admired the exterior of the large three-storeyed terraced property with something akin to amazement. She actually owned it! She still had difficulty taking in her good fortune. She just wished she had met her aunt and spent some time getting to know her. She must have been very lonely, living in such a huge place.

Seacrest was far too large for her and

Thomas to live in on their own — but what else could she do with it? She really didn't want to sell it. It would somehow feel like a betrayal of her aunt, who had apparently loved and cared for it all her life.

Annabel took out the key and unlocked the solid oak front door. It opened onto a wide, tiled hallway, with various doors leading off, and a kitchen at the far end. She wandered round the ground floor rooms absent-mindedly, absorbing the calm, peaceful atmosphere, and trying to imagine all the possibilities. There were four large bedrooms on the first floor, and four attics which had also been used for sleeping in. On the ground floor there were two large sitting rooms, a small dining room, a large kitchen, a walk-in pantry, and a cloakroom.

Most of the rooms were full of furniture, ornaments, and bric-a-brac, which were not generally to her taste. No doubt lots were very valuable, she supposed, so she would need advice about those. She did contemplate asking Luke's opinion, but was loath to do so. She wanted to stand on her own two feet as much as possible, so that even if she did make mistakes, she would only have herself to blame.

Having visited every room to savour the atmosphere, she ended up in the vast old-fashioned kitchen. It badly needed updating. How could her aunt have coped with the ancient black range and stone sink? It was like being in a time warp, and reminded Annabel in some ways of her unhappy time with Percy Wylde. She quickly blanked that out of her mind. She never wanted to think about Holly Bush Farm ever again.

She opened the back door that led out onto a paved yard, plus various outbuildings still to be investigated, but decided to leave them for another day. Thankfully, she wouldn't have to make any quick decisions. But she did want to move in some time soon, and make a start on clearing out all the cupboards and drawers. It would be lovely to be in her own home with her son, but she still didn't know how that could be achieved without a great deal of upset.

Finally, she locked up and walked back into town to do some Christmas shopping, her mind in a flurry of plans and ideas. It felt strange to be able to buy lots of presents and not worry about the cost, and in some ways she felt guilty for being extravagant.

At dinner that night, Luke announced that he'd had a letter from Jon to say he would be joining them for an extended Christmas holiday.

'Is he coming alone?' Jane asked. 'I thought Patsy said Christmas was a particularly busy time for them.'

'Yes, he'll be alone,' Luke said, frowning thoughtfully. Cautiously, he added, 'I think maybe he won't be in a hurry to return to France, if I'm not very much mistaken. Reading between the lines, I surmise that married life isn't exactly suiting him, and perhaps a divorce is in the offing.'

'Oh dear, so soon,' said Jane. 'I can't say I'm surprised, though. I wonder what Patsy's parents will think? When Jon was here for the funeral, I got the impression he and Patsy were not getting on too well. Whatever will he do?'

'He needn't think he's going to loaf around here,' snapped Robert. 'You'll have to find him some work to do, Luke, to keep him out of mischief. He's always been a idle blighter.'

Jane smiled, Luke sighed, and Annabel looked scared. As soon as she could, she escaped to her room to ponder on the latest turn of events. What would Jon say when he saw Thomas? Would he put two and two together? Should she go and tell Luke the truth straight away, and put an end to the uncertainty? With a monumental sigh, she decided not to be impetuous, but to wait until she'd slept on it. She knew she was just postponing the inevitable, because something had to be done and soon.

Annabel managed to get Jane on her

own after breakfast the following morning.

'What am I to do?' she asked. 'I do so want to sort out Seacrest, but I can't leave without Thomas. I can't bear to be separated from him.'

'Yes, of course. I understand,' replied Jane. She looked uncomfortable. 'I suppose there's not much point in delaying the inevitable any longer. Goodness knows what Luke will say, but perhaps now isn't such a bad time. He seems to be getting along very nicely with Caroline, and if my suspicions are correct and they marry eventually, Caroline won't want much to do with Thomas. I can't see her wanting to look after someone else's child, can you?'

Annabel didn't know what to say. She found Caroline Harker pleasant enough, but certainly didn't envisage her having control of Thomas. 'She would make Luke a good wife, I think,' she said quietly.

Jane nodded. She had been hoping

for a different outcome. She had prayed Lucas would look favourably on Annabel as wife material, but that wasn't to be. That would have been so much easier, especially since Annabel was now an heiress in her own right. 'Come, let us go and find Luke and confess all. I must say, I have been dreading this; so the sooner it's over and done, with the better.'

They found him in the library, wandering round the extensive shelving. 'Well done, Annabel,' he said. 'You've worked wonders. Father is very pleased.'

'We have something to talk to you about, Luke,' said Jane. 'It's rather delicate. Is now a good time?'

'Of course, of course. Come and sit down by the fire. Nothing wrong, is there?'

Annabel sat nervously on the edge of her seat and gazed at the flickering flames. Jane took a seat nearby, while Luke sat in a chair opposite and smiled encouragingly.

'Now, what can I do for you? You look worried. Is Father . . . ?'

'No, it's not Robert. Look, this is extremely difficult,' Jane said, clutching her hands together. 'I do wish things could have been different. You've had a lot to put up with this year, and we didn't want to add to your problems. The thing is . . . well . . . it's about Thomas.'

'Nothing wrong with the little fellow, is there?' Luke said quickly. 'I'm sorry I haven't spent much time with him recently. I'm afraid I have been occupied elsewhere.' He had the grace to flush with embarrassment.

'Thomas is fine,' said Annabel. 'Teething, which makes him a bit fractious, that's all. I thought you ought to know . . . well, the thing is . . . '

Luke looked from one to the other quizzically. 'Come on, spit it out.'

'Thomas is actually Annabel's son,' Jane said quickly.

There was a long pause before Luke responded. He looked incredulously at both of them. 'You're not joking . . . I don't understand. How is it possible . . . ?'

Jane settled back in her chair now the deed had been done. 'I'm so sorry, Luke, but it is true. It happened like this. Roxanne and I were out one day, and met Annabel, on her way here after the Christmas holiday. She came complete with a baby in a pram. Unfortunately, before we had chance to speak, Roxy's horse reared up and knocked Annabel into the river. She suffered amnesia. While she was convalescing, Roxanne came up with the idea of adopting Annabel's baby. She knew you wanted a son, and she thought she could give the baby a good start in life.'

'You mean she simply took Annabel's baby without asking?' Luke growled despairingly.

Jane nodded. 'I'm afraid so. She honestly did think it was for the best.' She didn't want to malign Roxanne now she was dead, so tried to make her sound benevolent. She turned to

Annabel. 'Roxy assumed the baby was yours; and, knowing you weren't married, knew you would have a difficult time bringing up a child alone. I did try to reason with her, really I did, but as usual she wouldn't listen. You know what she was like. Once she had a bee in her bonnet, there was no shifting her. I've been wanting to tell you . . . '

'I can't believe Roxy could be so . . . so wicked,' Luke said, looking absolutely horrified. 'And you say this baby is yours, Annabel? When . . . ? What happened?'

Biting her lip, Annabel took up the tale. She sidetracked away from who the father was, though. 'My memory suddenly came back while I was acting as a housekeeper to your Uncle Percy. I met a neighbour with a son called Tommy. The name clicked somehow.'

'Oh, for goodness' sake. I can't believe Roxy could do such a dreadful thing. She was a bit wild, I admit, but this is something quite appalling. I would never have countenanced such a thing. I can't believe she would . . . I do wish you had said something sooner.' Luke looked desperate. 'What are we going to do?'

'May I suggest we do nothing for the moment?' said Jane, quietly and calmly, sensing Luke's anguish. 'We just felt . . . in the present circumstances . . . that you ought to be told, that's all. Let's leave things be until after Christmas.'

Annabel remained quiet, not wanting to cause further upset, but desperately wanting to escape to Seacrest. She didn't want to meet Jon.

'Yes, yes, of course,' agreed Luke. 'This has taken me completely by surprise. Give me time for it to sink in, will you? Although, come to think of it, I should have suspected something was wrong when Roxanne couldn't produce any paperwork. I kept asking her for it, but she avoided it as usual. Somehow, this year . . . I've been . . . ' He shook his head. 'I'm so sorry, Annabel. We'll sort something out. We'll do whatever is in Thomas's best interests. That's all that matters. I'm so dreadfully sorry my wife could do such a thing to you.'

Annabel escaped before she could be questioned about Tommy's father. Later that day, she had a brainwave. She would invite the Palmers to stay with her for Christmas at Seacrest. Mrs Palmer would be a great help with clearing out her aunt's clothes, and perhaps Mr Palmer would be able to give her some suggestions about the garden. Surely she could make Seacrest liveable-in for a few days, even if it would feel rather primitive. Her aunt had lived there, for goodness' sake; and although it wasn't in Chellow Hall's league, it was — or would be, eventually — an impressive place.

When she next saw Luke, she told him what she planned; although he appeared reluctant, he did see the merit in what she proposed. He even agreed she could take Thomas with her. Annabel knew Miss Harker had been invited to spend Christmas at the Hall, so Lucas would be otherwise occupied anyway. Annabel was greatly relieved, and set about marshalling her thoughts as to what she would need to procure. Time was getting short.

★ ★ ★

The Palmers arrived by train two days before Christmas. Annabel was so pleased to see them, and they expressed delight at seeing Thomas so grown-up. She had spent a good deal of the last few days making Seacrest House as festive as she could, and on the whole, she didn't think it looked too bad.

'Why, it's enormous,' exclaimed Mrs Palmer on seeing the house, hardly able to contain her astonishment. 'Whatever will you do with all these rooms? It'll cost a bonny penny in upkeep, that's for sure.'

Annabel grinned. 'I welcome any suggestions, but first let's get you installed, and we'll chat later. I'm just so please you agreed to come.'

184

It was a wonderful Christmas, especially as it was Thomas's first and he was getting very active. He'd begun to crawl, and was even trying to walk, although he wasn't talking yet except for the odd garbled word now and again. As she had expected when she asked the Palmers if they would care to come and live with her, they reluctantly declined. They'd spent all their lives in London, and had no wish to leave their tiny two-bedroomed house. They were delighted to learn Annabel was comfortably off now, and that Thomas was doing so well. Their only disappointment was that his father wasn't in evidence. Annabel assured them she was perfectly happy with the way things were, and said that if she ever did consider getting married, they would be the first to hear.

All too soon, the Palmers left. Annabel and Thomas waved them off on the train, and returned to Seacrest to clear up. She had hoped they would stay for New Year's Day, but they declined, saying that they always spent it in their own home, and wished to ring in the new year the way they had always done.

New Year. What should she do for New Year? Should she go back to Chellow Hall and face meeting Jon again? No — she couldn't bear for Jon to see Thomas and put two and two together. She would spend it quietly in her own home, and felt sure Lucas would understand. She had plenty to occupy herself with, sorting out the contents of her home and keeping Thomas out of mischief.

On New Year's Eve, she decided she might as well have an early night. There really didn't seem much point in sitting up just to see the new year in by herself. She had started making some cocoa when the doorbell rang.

She glanced at the clock. It was gone ten. Who on earth could it be? Still in a simple dress and cardigan, she rather reluctantly went to answer the door, hoping it wasn't one of her neighbours since she wasn't in a party mood. She wasn't sure what the people of Scarborough did in that way of celebrating New Year, but didn't want to appear inhospitable. She was stunned to see Jon on the doorstep, waving a bottle of wine.

'I've been hearing all about your wonderful news, and couldn't bear the thought of you sitting here all alone on such an auspicious night.'

She nearly said she wasn't alone, but then wondered cautiously what he'd been told. Did he know about Thomas? She opened the door wider, hoping and praying Thomas wouldn't wake up. Recently he had been sleeping through the night.

'It's lovely to see you, Jon, but surely you haven't driven twenty miles just to wish me a Happy New Year?'

'Why ever not? What's twenty miles between friends? We are friends, aren't we?' He grinned, muscling his way into the hallway. 'I've missed you, Annie. Christmas was awfully dull without you. Father gave me a telling-off as usual, and Luke seems to be mesmerised by a certain rather haughty lady called Caroline, and made me feel I was playing gooseberry.'

Annabel laughed and showed him into the room she was using as a sitting room. 'You're married,' she said quietly, and went to put another log on the fire, fiercely poking it to life. 'Why didn't Patsy come with you?'

'Hmm,' he replied, glancing around the cosy room. 'Big mistake, my marriage. Didn't work out, but I'm going to rectify that before long.'

'Oh,' she said, retrieving some glasses from the sideboard and handing Jon the corkscrew. 'How will you manage that?'

'I'll think of something, never fear — but not let's talk about such dismal subjects. Let's talk about you and your inheritance. I want to know all you've been doing since I last saw you.'

Annabel murmured that there wasn't much to tell him, and hoped he would change the subject. After opening the wine, Jon settled on the settee, and grinned as Annabel took a chair some distance away.

'Cheers. I've changed, Annabel, I really have. I know I've been a stupid pillock, but if Dad and Luke will give me a chance, I want to show them I'm capable of doing something useful about the estate. Luke has far too much to do now that Father has more or less retired, and I've got all sorts of ideas — one of which is to expand the stables and set up a riding school.'

'Sounds like a good idea. What does Patsy have to say to that?'

'To be quite honest, I don't care a fig what she says. I should never have married her. The marriage was doomed from the start. I only did it because . . . well, you probably know why. It was Father's idea to save the family name from being dragged through the mud. Patsy got the kudos of being a Wylde of Chellow Hall, and I had my gambling debts paid.'

He gazed at her sadly and poured

more wine, while she thought again how attractive he was. He still had that casual, easy-going manner Luke lacked; but he also looked tired, and older than his years.

Raising his glass, he said, 'To you, Annie, my love. May the new year prove to be much, much better than this last one!'

She lifted her glass and smiled. 'This last year hasn't been all bad.'

'I'm pleased to hear it, because from what Jane told me, you've had quite a tough time of it one way and another.'

Annabel wasn't used to drinking, and soon her head was swimmy. *Surely he won't want to stay until midnight*, she thought. How could she tactfully get him to go? *Please, God, don't let Thomas cry out . . .*

Jon spent the best part of the next couple of hours sprawled on the settee, reminiscing and joking and making her laugh. It felt so good to laugh. She had missed Jon, more than she had realised. Before, she had been in awe of him and his superior family; but now she felt relaxed, and found herself telling him about her worries concerning the house she had inherited.

'I could help you there,' he said promptly. 'I know a thing or two about antiques and so forth.'

Annabel nodded. 'That's very kind. I'll let you know.'

When distant church bells announced the New Year, Jon stood and pulled her into his arms before she had a chance to object. He bent to kiss her and murmured, 'Happy New Year, Annie. Here's to your wonderful future.' She nuzzled against him, feeling totally bewitched. *I've had far too much wine*, she thought. *I shouldn't be doing this. Jon is still a married man, despite what he says about Patsy.*

'I guess I had better be going,' he whispered, sounding sorrowful.

Part of her wanted him to stay, but instead she acquiesced and thanked him for coming. 'Take care,' she said as she saw him out the door. With another brief kiss on her cheek, he departed, and she listened to the roar of his car engine as it disappeared into the night.

Jane arrived the next morning as Annabel was about to start packing. She was lethargic and heavy-headed, so not feeling too sociable.

'Hello, Annabel. I hoped I'd catch you in.'

Annabel led her into the sitting room where Thomas was in his playpen. 'Would you like some coffee?'

'Oh, yes please,' Jane replied, bending over to pick up Thomas, who gurgled happily. 'I won't stay long, but I came on behalf of Luke, actually.' She followed Annabel into the kitchen. 'Luke suggests you keep Thomas here for the time being if that suits you.'

Annabel turned round with startled eyes.

Jane laughed. 'It's probably something to do with Miss Harker. She has spent Christmas and New Year enter- taining — or being entertained by

— Luke. She has certainly got her claws into him, so much so that Luke is looking totally bemused. I'm not sure whether it's a good thing or not. Caroline can be a bit forthright . . . but that's no bad thing overall, is it?'

'So I can keep Thomas, and there will be no repercussions?' Annabel said, surprised.

'It would appear so. However, I must also tell you that Luke is speculating as to who his father is. He thinks the man responsible ought to be made to pay maintenance.'

Annabel bit her lip and turned to deal with the kettle. 'I don't want any help from him,' she stated coldly. 'I've managed alone so far, and that's the way I like it. Come; let's go and sit in the front room by the fire. It's much warmer there. I shall be glad when I can get someone in to modernise this kitchen.'

'Don't worry, Annabel. Luke won't make trouble, and neither will I. Obviously, there has been much speculation

. . . Now, I understand you had a visit from Jon last night. I'm afraid he was getting bored with the company at the Hall, especially as my husband still can't recognise how he's changed. I said all along Patsy wasn't the wife for him. I, for one, am delighted he's back. He's very good with Sophie, too; she thinks the world of him.'

'He only came to wish me a Happy New Year,' Annabel said quietly, and quickly changed the subject. 'Actually, he told me of his plans — about the riding stable, etcetera. He even offered to help me decide what to do with this house's contents.'

Jane put Thomas back in his playpen and accepted the coffee. 'That's a good idea, but I wonder what Patsy will think? Jon does need something to get his teeth into, though, and you do need a hand with all this. It's quite a task you've taken on.'

'I know,' sighed Annabel. 'I keep changing my mind about what to do with it. It's far too big for me to live in alone, and I won't sell it. I had at one stage thought of turning it into flats, but then I read some of my aunt's diaries and found out she ran it as a small guesthouse before the war. So I think that might be the way to go. It would be more ongoing work for me, obviously, and I'm not sure if I want that. I tried to persuade the Palmers to join me, but they wish to spend their retirement in London. Didn't you once live in London?'

Jane nodded. 'Yes, but I've no wish to go back there. I couldn't wait to leave. I know Chellow Hall isn't to everyone's liking, and I know I really shouldn't say this . . . but it is much more agreeable since Roxanne passed away. She was often bored, and did outrageous things, and somehow always managed to involve me in her madcap schemes. Now I feel as if I've got my life back, so I do hope Caroline Harker doesn't prove to be like her. I don't think I could bear it.'

Annabel smiled her understanding.

* * *

Jon arrived out of the blue one morning. 'You know, you ought to see about getting the telephone installed. I could have let you know I was coming.'

And I could have told you I was busy, she thought. She knew Jon would have to see Thomas one day, but was scared about his reaction. Thomas was becoming more like his father every day, and she wondered if anyone else saw the likeness.

'How about you showing me round your home,' Jon said, 'and then we can discuss your proposals.'

'I haven't had time to formulate any proposals as yet,' she said, her mind in a whirl. Thomas was in his playpen, but she couldn't leave him there alone while they walked round the house. She didn't think Jon would leave soon enough for to avoid him seeing Thomas, so with a sigh, she led him into the sitting room.

'Oh, who have we here?' Jon said,

going over, then picking up and waggling Thomas's teddy. 'I wondered where Luke's son had gone. I guess you were given the job of looking after him while he is otherwise busy.'

Annabel looked at him in surprise. Had nobody told him? What was she to do? One of these days he would find out he was Thomas's father, for sure.

'Thomas is my son,' she said quietly.

Jon stood, and looked first at her, then at Thomas, clearly stunned. 'Yours?'

'Yes,' she said, and went to pick Thomas up. 'I thought Jane would have told you.'

Jon still looked mystified.

Annabel took a deep breath. 'Thomas is mine, but I had an accident and had amnesia. Roxanne decided to adopt him without my knowledge. Luke didn't know Thomas was mine until just before Christmas. Roxanne hadn't told him.'

Jon was staring at Thomas as if not believing what he was seeing. 'Am I missing something here?'

Annabel shrugged her shoulders.

'Yours . . . and *mine*?'

She nodded.

With a whoosh of breath, he threw himself down on the settee. 'Why am I the last to find out?'

'I haven't told anyone who Thomas's father is,' she snapped. 'It's nobody else's business.'

Jon shook his head in disbelief. 'Surely . . . you only have to look at him to see . . . see the likeness.'

'I think your family were too sensitive about my feelings to say anything, even if they did guess.'

'Oh, Annie, why on earth didn't you tell me?'

'Because I only found out I was pregnant after you were married. Look, I don't want any hassle, Jon. I just want to live quietly here with my son and get on with my life.'

'He's my son too!' he cried. 'Surely I should have some say in the matter?'

'But, I repeat, you are *married* — to

Patsy. You were still on your honeymoon when I found out, I think — so what was I to do? Look, now you know you have a son, fine — but as far as I'm concerned, he's my responsibility. I'll take good care of him. After all, he's all I have.'

Jon rose from the settee. 'I need time to think. I can't get my head round this. But I promise you this, Annie — I won't be an absent father. I promise you.' With that, he stormed out of the house.

15

Would she see Jon again? Oh yes, no doubt she would. It's a pity he hadn't heard the full version of her story, but he had looked totally shell-shocked as it was. Thinking about it, she could understand how astonishing it must have been for him. He had obviously had no idea that Annabel even had a child — his child — but she still felt she had been right not to tell him. It could make things difficult for him if he went ahead with the divorce he was contemplating . . .

Well, that was for him to sort out; she still had so much to deal with. Apart from organising having a telephone installed, she wanted to get started on the kitchen refurbishment as a priority. The present one seemed so depressing, with its old-fashioned range and stone sink. She had seen an advertisement in the local paper for a general handyman and arranged for him to call.

He arrived one evening; looking rather scruffy, so she was a little wary. 'Steve Johnson. Sorry for arriving looking like this,' he apologised. 'I've just finished for the day and haven't had time to go home and change. You said it was urgent.'

Annabel grinned. She liked the sound of his voice, and was pleased he had apologised for his appearance. 'Do come in, Mr Johnson. I'm afraid the place is in a bit of a mess, but I suppose you are used to that.' She led him through to the kitchen. 'I'm not sure if this is the sort of work you do, but . . . well, I desperately want a new kitchen.'

He smiled. 'I see what you mean.'

Annabel wasn't sure what to do next, so she offered him coffee while they discussed possibilities.

'That would be great.'

He took out a notebook and looked about while Annabel set about finding mugs and coffee. 'What had you in mind? This looks like a big job. These old house are so substantial, but it gives you plenty of scope.'

They sat at the kitchen table and she explained her situation. 'I inherited the house, but it's too big for me to take on all at once, so I thought I would make a start with the ground floor. I'd like to make it into a self-contained flat. Later on, if I get some inspiration, the upper floors would make nice flats too, I think. The last owner used to take in visitors, I believe.'

'Yes, that's right. I remember Miss Broom. She was a dear old soul. The story was, her fiancé was killed in the war — that would be the First World War. For the rest of her life, she and her parents worked this place as a guesthouse; and when they died, she carried on, but it gradually became too much for her. She shut herself off, and lived frugally with just cats for company. At least, that was what the local gossip-mongers said.'

'I wonder what happened to the cats?' Annabel said. 'Maybe now I'm here, they will return. Anyway, back to the plan. Do you think you can help me?'

'It would cost a bonny penny, but certainly I could install a new kitchen for you, no problem.'

'I've been told it's going to cost a fair bit to bring it up to scratch, so I'm quite prepared for that. The thing is, the house is too big for me and my son, but I don't want to sell it. Miss Broom entrusted it to me, and I feel honour-bound to stay, at least for the time being. I just wish I had met my benefactor.'

'Look, if you are really sure you want me to do it, I'd be happy to do so. I know other trades I could employ as and when necessary. Estimating the job would be a little tricky, though. Have you approached anyone else? You should, you know.'

She shook her head. 'I don't want the hassle. Will you do the kitchen for me?

Then we'll see how we go after that.'

'You're very trusting.'

She shrugged her shoulders. 'I just hope you won't let me down then.'

⋆ ⋆ ⋆

Two weeks later, the doorbell rang. 'Jon,' she exclaimed cautiously. She had been a little surprised — and, to be honest, disappointed — that he hadn't been in touch again. 'How are you?' She led him through to the nearly-completed kitchen, where Steve was having a tea-break and cuddling Thomas.

Jon frowned angrily.

'This is Steve,' Annabel said, quietly retrieving Thomas. 'As you can see, he's been remodelling the kitchen for me.'

Jon nodded. 'Can I have a word . . . in private?'

'Yes, of course. Let's go into the front room.'

'What was he doing with Thomas?' Jon demanded.

'Keeping him out of mischief — what did you think? Thomas is into everything now, and Steve has been very patient with him. Not that it is any of your business . . . So, what did you want to speak to me about?'

'Us, of course.'

'What exactly do you mean? *Us?*'

He went over to the fireplace and watched as Annabel put Thomas in his playpen. He shoved his hands in his pockets and frowned. 'I want us to be a family, Annie. I love you. I always have. Marrying Patsy was a mistake. Now, having found out I have a son, you mean more to me than ever.'

'But you are still married to Patsy. How can we be a family? Even if that was what I wanted . . . '

He looked annoyed with her for interrupting.

'I just thought . . . you do love me, don't you?'

'I don't know what I want right now, except to be left in peace. I don't think there is any point in continuing this discussion, Jon. You need to sort your own life out — with Patsy. Thomas will be here if you want to see him, but I am rather busy at the moment, as you can see.'

'I thought I was going to help you with the refurbishment?'

She sighed. 'I got tired of that miserable kitchen, especially now Thomas is getting much more mobile. I just wanted the ground floor arranging as a comfortable, self-contained flat, then later on I'll decide whether to turn the upstairs into more flats to rent out. I could certainly do with some assistance at that stage, but for the moment I've got my hands full.'

'I see. Your plans don't include me, then?'

'I'm sorry, Jon. Really, I am. And at some stage I would like Thomas to know you are his father . . . but you have to admit, things are rather complicated. I had a fairly strict upbringing, so I have no wish to be named as 'the other woman' if you and Patsy do decide to divorce; and I certainly don't believe in living with another woman's husband.'

He sighed, and shook his head miserably. 'I do understand, honestly I do, but I was so thrilled to learn I have a son. He's so gorgeous. Somehow, I've got to find a way out of this mess.'

16

Lady Jane arrived unexpectedly. Annabel was getting used to people dropping in, and she proudly showed them the newly-renovated kitchen. 'What do you think?' she said.

'It's a wonderful improvement,' Jane said, taking in the lovely light and airy room's new cupboards, sink and electrical gadgets. 'You must be extremely pleased with it.'

Annabel smiled and went to put the kettle on. 'I have Steve to thank for it. He took me to all the right places, and helped me choose the new equipment. I'm really thrilled with it all. He's now making a start on a downstairs cloakroom for me.' She noticed that Jane seemed preoccupied. 'Have you come to Scarborough for something specific?'

'Well, I was wanting to ask a favour

of you. A huge favour, actually. I don't know if you heard that Patsy was involved in an accident?'

'Oh, no! What happened?' Annabel said, placing coffee and shortbread on the table and giving Thomas a rusk.

Jane slumped down a chair and rested her head in her hands. 'It would appear she was in London on business and was robbed. Unfortunately, instead of letting the thief get away with her handbag like most people would, she tackled him and ended up with concussion. She's been in hospital for nearly a week, and I'm afraid things aren't looking good. To begin with, nobody knew who she was, since she had no identification on her and she hadn't let anyone know she was in London except Jon. He went down to be with her, and then flew to France to see to the business. I was rather hoping, since you have friends in London, whether you felt like going down to assist Jon. I know it's asking a lot, but there's nobody else . . . '

Annabel looked dismayed. 'But I'm in the middle of the refurbishment. I don't see how I can.'

'I know I'm asking a lot, Annabel, but Jon really does need someone to hold his hand, and I just thought in the circumstances, it would give you time to . . . well, just . . . you know. I'm afraid I can't leave Robert, and Lucas is up to his eyes in work as usual. I'm sorry if you feel it's an imposition, but I thought . . . '

'Yes, I see,' said Annabel, flushing with embarrassment. 'So I take it Jon told you he's Thomas's father.'

Jane looked guilty. 'I admit, I guessed; but, yes, he told me. He was thrilled to bits. Thomas looks so much like Jon, you know. He has his eyes, and of course the lovely red hair. He really is gorgeous, and looks a true Wylde, doesn't he?'

Annabel nodded ruefully. Thomas didn't seem to take after her at all. 'I really don't know what to do — about Jon. I don't know much about his marriage or anything, but I am sorry to hear about Patsy. From what I remember, she wasn't likely to let go of her property without a fight.'

'She is rather a domineering female,' Jane said ruefully.

Annabel gave a great sigh. 'What exactly did you want me to do?'

'Well, I thought perhaps you could you visit your friends the Palmers, and maybe have them look after Thomas while you do some hospital visiting? I know you won't want to leave Thomas at the Hall, will you?'

'No, I don't think so. I want to keep him with me, especially as now he's beginning to say a few words. I don't want to miss any of his growing-up. The Palmers, I'm sure, would be only too pleased to have me stay with them, and would happily babysit. All right, I'll go, as long as Steve is content to carry on here working without me. Come to think of it, he'll probably be pleased not to have Thomas's input!'

'Lively, is he?'

'Into everything as soon as your back's turned. He has a passion for Steve's toolbox.'

* * *

Fortunately, Steve was agreeable to working on alone, and even said he would try to complete the cloakroom for her return. A telegram was dispatched to the Palmers, and they responded promptly by saying they would be delighted for Annabel to visit, so it was soon arranged for Pettigrew to transport her and Thomas to London. She had suggested going by train, but soon realised how much luggage she needed for them both, so accepted the lift gratefully. She tried to keep all thoughts of Jon out of her mind, although it wasn't easy when every day Thomas looked so much like him. She had trouble keeping Thomas amused on the long journey to London, so by the time they arrived she was exhausted.

The next day, she paid a visit to the hospital, but unfortunately Jon wasn't there: he was still in France, apparently. Patsy, when she was finally admitted to her bedside, was comatose. She was in a ward by herself and attached to all sorts of paraphernalia that Annabel found most disturbing. She sat at her bedside for a little while, wondering what Patsy would think when she heard Jon had a son. Would she sue for divorce? She had only ever seen Patsy once before, and that was from a distance so she really didn't think there was much point in her waiting around for long. According to the nurse she saw as she was leaving, they were expecting Mr Wylde to visit later that afternoon, so Annabel decided to go for a walk round and return later. She finally met Jon outside the hospital, where he was having a quiet smoke.

'Hello, Jon,' she said softly. 'How are you?'

He shrugged his shoulders and put out his cigarette. 'Could be better, as the saying goes. I suppose Jane sent you?'

She nodded. 'She rather thought you could do with some moral support, and I was nominated. So, what can I do to help? I have never been introduced to Patsy, so I really don't know what help I can be.'

He sighed. 'To be quite honest, Annie, I'm just pleased to see you. I really am. I need someone to talk to, because I don't think Patsy is going to pull through.'

'Oh, no!' she cried, suitably horrified. 'I didn't realise it was so bad. I am so sorry.'

He turned to look back at the hospital entrance. 'I'll just go and show my face and see if there has been any change, and then I'll be back. Perhaps we can go somewhere to talk.'

'Yes, of course. I'll wait here.'

He was back within ten minutes and took her by the arm. 'Patsy's folks are with her. So, have you had anything to eat? I'm starving. I know of a little place not far away, would that be all right?'

Seated in a small restaurant, Annabel asked what had actually happened.

'From what the police have told me, it rather looks as if Patsy was attacked shortly after leaving me.' He frowned thoughtfully. 'I got in touch with her as soon as I could after I learned about Thomas. I said I needed to see her urgently, and she told me she was going to be in London, viewing a proposed new hotel investment. So I agreed to meet her one evening at a restaurant in Kensington — her choice, as usual. Anyway, we hadn't got beyond our first drinks when we ended up arguing, as we were prone to do, and she stormed out.

'By the time I had paid the bill and collected my coat, there was no sign of her outside. I assumed she had been lucky and got a taxi, but it would appear she was being her usual foolish self and had decided to walk back to her hotel. Somewhere on the way, she was accosted and had her handbag snatched; but, rather than let the thief take it, she fought back, the stupid woman. She was discovered unconscious at the bottom of some steps near the park some time later.'

'How distressing.'

'The police have questioned me at length, of course, and made me feel guilty for not escorting her, but she could be so damned perverse. Anyone who knew her would know that there was no reasoning with her when she was in a mood.'

'What were you arguing about?'

'Oh, everything from how to run a hotel to us getting a divorce. Look, I'm sorry Jane involved you, but I am grateful for your company, Annie. I don't know whether I'm on my head or my heels. Patsy's parents have been giving me a hard time, too. They are blaming me, of course. I get the blame for everything these days.'

'Surely not? How can you be held responsible for Patsy's actions? I know I wouldn't walk anywhere in London after dark alone. Patsy should have got a taxi like you said. There are usually plenty about, and the restaurant would possibly have got one for her if she'd asked.'

He stretched across and took her hand. 'Bless you, Annie. At least you have some common sense. I can always rely on you for that.'

'What exactly do you want me to do?' she said, pulling her hand away. She really didn't want to get involved in their disagreements. She wasn't even sure if she wanted much to do with Jon in the future, no matter what he thought to the contrary. Obviously, he would want occasional contact with his son, but she didn't think that would amount to much. At least, not based on his past behaviour, it wouldn't.

He sighed. 'If you wouldn't mind sitting with Patsy each morning, I'd really appreciate it. I know it seems superfluous since she just lies there, but I wouldn't want her to wake and find nobody around. Her parents generally spend the afternoon with her, so I go each evening.'

Annabel nodded. 'The Palmers have offered to look after Thomas, so that shouldn't be a problem; but how can I reach you if she does wake up? After all, she won't know me. I'm like a stranger to her.'

'I'll leave you a phone number where you can reach me; and that of her parents too. They want to be contacted if there is any change in her condition, of course.' He sighed again wearily. 'From what the specialist told me, they don't hold out much hope of her recovering consciousness. She banged her head on the edge of the stone steps, so even if she does wake up, there will probably be brain damage.'

'I'm so sorry, Jon. This must all be terribly difficult for you, especially as you parted on such bad terms. I will do what I can to help, of course, don't worry.'

Jon took hold of her hand again and stroked it very gently. 'Where did we go wrong, Annie? I should never have let you get away.'

She snatched her hand away as if she'd been burned, and shrugged. 'Don't be silly. There never was any *we*. You know as well as I do that you never had any intention of marrying me. It was just one of your casual flings. I didn't have money in those days, remember?'

He looked a bit taken aback at her retort. 'I know I treated you badly, and I am sorry, but I promise I'm a reformed character now. I've learned my lesson the hard way. When Patsy recovers — *if* she recovers — I'll make her see sense and get a divorce. We should never have married in the first place.'

Annabel looked at him, thinking about the fun times, and then took a deep breath. 'I did love you, and at the time I thought you loved me . . . but I soon realised that, to you, I was just another dumb, naïve simpleton, overwhelmed by the great Jonathon Wylde's charisma. Fortunately, I too have learned my lesson, and won't be taken in quite so easily by any man in future. I'm in no hurry to walk down the aisle.'

'You know,' he said grimly, 'all my life I have been competing with Lucas and failing badly. From the early days, Luke knew he was destined to take over Chellow Hall. I never knew what I would do. He sailed through school and got top marks without really trying, while I struggled all the way. My mother used to appease me by saying how good I was at playing the piano and sports and suchlike, whereas Luke excelled in the academic subjects. When I left school, Mother used to have me play for her social gatherings, and I sort of accepted my role there. I know my father thinks I'm a waste of space, but in his eyes, speaking foreign languages count for nothing in the great scheme of things. They certainly aren't needed to run the estate.'

'We can't all be good at everything. I suppose we both feel we have let our parents down, don't we?'

'Not you, sweetheart. Your parents would be immensely proud of your success.'

She grimaced. 'Anyway, that is all beside the point.' She glanced at her watch. 'I must be getting back. I don't want Thomas wearing the Palmers out.'

He signalled for the bill. 'Thank you for coming, Annie. It has done me a power of good just having someone to talk to. Someone hopefully on my side.'

*   *   *

Two days later, Annabel was about to go to the hospital when Jon arrived at the Palmers' house. She could tell from the look on his face that it wasn't good news.

'Patsy died early this morning without recovering consciousness,' he said as she led him into the small front room. He immediately slumped in an armchair and held his head in his hands.

She feared he was crying, and didn't know what to do or say. Eventually, she put her hand on his shoulder. 'I'm sorry, Jon, but in a way it may have been a blessing — if, as you said, there could have been brain damage. I don't suppose she would have wanted to live in those circumstances. I know I wouldn't.'

He nodded. He looked shattered.

'Have you been at the hospital all night? You look all in.'

He nodded again.

'Can I get you some breakfast? We can talk in the kitchen; the Palmers have taken Thomas out for a while.'

'What am I going to do?' he said with a monumental sigh, taking a seat at the table while Annabel busied herself cooking eggs and bacon.

'You mean, with the funeral and so on?'

'No, that at least her parents are taking care of. No, I mean the business. Patsy's hotel in the south of France, for a start.'

'I guess it's yours now, as her next of kin, isn't it?'

'I suppose so. I've no idea.'

17

'Oh, Lucas. I'm sorry, I didn't know anyone was in here.' Jane went over to the chest of drawers and replaced some clothing. She glanced across at Luke, who was sitting looking pensively out of the nursery window. 'Are you all right?' she asked cautiously.

He nodded. 'Sure.'

'It's rather quiet around here these days, isn't it?' She frowned. 'I do so miss Thomas and Annabel.'

'Yes,' sighed Luke. 'I do too.'

'I haven't seen Caroline recently. Is she . . . ? Are you . . . ?'

'I think I found her rather trying over Christmas, if the truth be known,' he replied, playing idly with a small teddy he'd picked up off the floor. 'If you must know, I miss Thomas more than I would ever have imagined. I used to love visiting him each evening, even if it was only for half an hour before his bedtime. I wish Annabel hadn't taken him away.'

Jane went to stand next to Luke. 'Is it just Thomas you're missing, Luke?' she asked softly.

He sighed deeply. 'Is it so obvious? Ever since the first time Jon brought Annabel to work here, I've been attracted to her. She's some special young lady. I kept my feelings under wraps because I was married . . . Roxanne was my wife, and of course I loved her; but I couldn't help but notice Annabel's innate calm, tranquil disposition, so very different from Roxanne's. I felt guilty then for having such feelings, but now . . . Anyway, Annabel perhaps has other suitors. You won't say anything, will you?'

'Of course I won't. What do you take me for? Anyhow, there's nothing to tell, is there? You've been a good, honest husband, who deserves someone at his side that understands his workload. Someone not quite so socially preoccupied, perhaps. The thing is ... maybe Annabel feels the same way about you? Have you thought about that? Now you are unencumbered so to speak she may find your company appealing?'

'Why would she? I know I'm rather a dull old stick compared to the likes of Jon — and it's Jon she seems attracted to, isn't it? After all, he is Thomas's father.'

Jane took hold of Luke's arm. 'That's as maybe; but Jon, as you know, is a bit of an extrovert, and that might not be what Annabel seeks. For the moment, all she is interested in is refurbishing her new home — and she is finding that exceedingly difficult, I might add. I had to twist her arm when it came to going to London: she really didn't want to go. She did it for me, not Jon.'

'Oh, I don't know. I feel like an old stick-in-the-mud compared to Jon, even though there's only three years between us.'

'You had all the responsibility thrust

on you that Jon never did; and you've done a remarkable job, too. I know your father grumbles from time to time and takes you to task, but actually he really is very proud of you, Luke. Don't run yourself down. I think, if you don't mind my saying so, Roxy was a difficult person to keep up with. I'm very sorry for what happened, but now it's time to move on.'

'You think so?' he said with a wistful sigh.

'I know so. Chellow needs more children to liven things up, and you are not getting any younger. Annabel is a lovely person, and what have you got to lose by asking her out? Now, I must go and see if Sophie has worn your father out. She's at the stage of asking questions all the time, and can be quite wearisome.'

He stood. 'Thanks, Jane. I appreciate your words of wisdom and woman's viewpoint. I'll think about what you've said. So you don't think Caroline fits the bill?' he added, with a wry smile.

Jane shrugged her shoulders. 'Not for me to lead your life for you, but she wouldn't be my choice. Of course, I'm prejudiced, because Annabel and I came from similar backgrounds.' With that, she left Lucas replacing toys and ruminating on what Jane had told him.

Was it because he was lonely he was thinking about Thomas — and Annabel? He hadn't been lonely at Christmas. If anything, he had been pursued almost every minute of the day until he had been almost desperate for some peace and quiet. Was it too soon to be thinking about getting married again? Marriage to Roxanne hadn't been easy, for sure, but he couldn't say it hadn't been lively. It had been like living on a volcano, wondering when it was going to erupt. He did miss her; but, on the other hand, he could see the attraction of Annabel. She liked the same things he did: books, reading, walks, music ... and, of course, children.

Annabel was relieved to be back in Scarborough. It was late by the time they pulled up outside Seacrest, and she was somewhat weary. She had enjoyed seeing the Palmers and being in London again, but the hospital visiting had been distressing, and she had been disturbed by Jon's behaviour. Once he had got over the shock of Patsy's death, he seemed more interested in getting back to business than mourning her. Had they really had such a bad relationship that he was glad she was dead? He certainly didn't seem as upset as Patsy's parents were. Being their only child, they were devastated she had died so young.

Annabel had been prepared to catch a train home, but when she telephoned Lucas to tell him about Patsy's death, he had insisted Pettigrew should be made available to bring her home whenever she was ready. In the event, she was extremely grateful as she had so much luggage, having done some shopping while she had time to spare.

Once Thomas was settled in his cot, she went to investigate what Steve had managed to do while she had been away. It was desperately cold in the flat, and wished she had taken Luke up on his offer of staying at the Hall for a while. Only stubbornness had made her determined to remain in Scarborough. The house really wasn't at all habitable in such cold conditions. She wasn't really needed to supervise Steve. He had a key to get in, and she was more than happy for him to work there while she was out.

She had thought that once the kitchen and cloakroom were modernised she would feel more comfortable, but somehow it still lacked something. She made her way to the cloakroom, hoping it would lift her spirits, and was delighted to find it extremely pleasing. Steve had worked wonders; she was so glad she had employed him. He had left a note telling her he wouldn't be around for a few days, since he had another client who needed him rather urgently. This suited Annabel, as it gave her time to decide what to do next.

After breakfast the next morning, she cleared away her clothes and began the washing. Then had to go shopping, as the pantry was bare. When she returned, she got a fire going and settled Thomas in his playpen. Then she got out pencil and paper and tried to plan her next move with the refurbishment. She was having difficulty concentrating; her mind kept wandering off in ways she wished it wouldn't.

She kept thinking about Jon, and exploring what her true feelings for him were — not that it mattered, as he would have his hands full for the next few months at least. The last she had heard, he was flying back to France, but would return to England for the funeral.

'Oh, Thomas, whatever shall I do?' she said, going to pick him up and giving him a cuddle. The front door bell rang. 'Now, who can that be?' she said with a chuckle as Thomas squealed with laughter.

'Lucas! How lovely to see you. Do come in. We're in here, where it's warm now I've got the fire going. I'd like to thank you for sending Pettigrew for me. It would have been a nightmare on the train. I really ought to learn to drive. What do you think? Oh, do sit down. I'm sorry; I'm gabbling, aren't I?'

He smiled and sat in the armchair. Thomas immediately went over and pulled himself up by grabbing onto Lucas's trousers. 'Hello, Thomas. My, aren't you a clever boy? Into everything, is he?'

'Oh, yes. That's why I trap him in the playpen occasionally, so I can get on with some work. Would you like something to drink?'

'No thank you, Annabel. I won't stay long, but I . . . I just wondered how you were managing in this cold weather. The forecast is for snow.'

'Well, it was a bit of a shock coming back last night, but we went straight to bed so it wasn't too bad. Steve — the man who's been doing the work — has finished for the time being, so I'm now trying to decide what to do next.'

Lucas picked up Thomas and settled him on his knee. 'I'm grateful to you for going to support Jon like you did, and I have a suggestion to make, which I hope you'll give serious consideration to. I do, by the way, think it would great if you had a car and could drive, so why don't you let Pettigrew teach you? There's the whole of Chellow's grounds at your disposal.'

'But how would I get to and fro? And, of course, there's Thomas to consider.'

'Oh, sorry. I should have said. The reason I came was to see if I could convince you to stay at the Hall — until the better weather, at least. There will be the funeral arrangements to attend to, and Jane was hoping you would assist her. What do you say? You would be doing me a real favour, actually. The Hall seems so very quiet these days.'

'I don't know what to say. It's very generous of you. You've done so much for me already. I don't want to become a nuisance . . . but I suppose I've come to an impasse for the moment, so I could spend some time there if it would help.' She frowned. 'Are you sure Pettigrew wouldn't mind teaching me? I should go to a driving school, but that would be difficult with Thomas. I would find life a lot more convenient if I could drive a car, though.'

'Right, that's settled,' Lucas said immediately, before she could change her mind. 'If you don't get on with Pettigrew, then I'll teach you, or Jane will. Perhaps we all will,' he added with a laugh.

Annabel privately wondered what Miss Harker would say.

★　★　★

Annabel arranged to go to Chellow Hall two days later, once she had talked to Steve and done some packing again. Thomas also needed more attention, as he seemed unsettled since they had returned from London, so she was feeling a bit hassled. Steve was again rather busy, so she agreed to contact him when she returned to Scarborough.

The morning after Luke's visit, she had a strange feeling that things were not where they were supposed to be around the flat. Little things, but still disturbing. She was sure someone had moved a chair — which in itself didn't matter, but part of a loaf of bread appeared to have gone too. A beaker was also missing. She couldn't find it anywhere. She was worried her amnesia was returning, but also felt positive that odd things were happening she couldn't account for. *Perhaps it's just as well I'm going back to the Hall*, she thought, getting worried about Thomas's safety.

Pettigrew once again was given the task of driving her and Thomas to

Chellow Hall, which he did with due formality. Teaching her to drive was not mentioned, so Annabel didn't raise the subject either. She was having second thoughts about having him teach her, and thought perhaps she should book into a driving school on her return to Scarborough. She had obtained a provisional driving licence, but was nervous about getting behind the wheel of a car, especially in her present state of mind.

'It's so good of you to come,' Jane said, giving her a hug, and Annabel felt she really meant it. 'We've missed you both.'

'Lucas twisted my arm in view of the snow forecast. I must admit, the refurbishment is taking more sorting-out than I had thought. I'm beginning to think I've taken on more than I can cope with.'

Jane nodded thoughtfully. 'I can well understand that. You do look tired, Annabel. I suppose the time in London was very upsetting and hasn't helped.'

'It had its moments,' she replied with a wry grin.

'Well, we'll have to see if you can get some rest while you're here. I don't suppose this little fellow gives you a minute's peace, so I'm glad we still have Rosie, who is dying to get reacquainted with him.'

★ ★ ★

A few days later Annabel was feeling much better. Not having to worry about anything helped restore her *joie de vivre*, so much so that when Jane suggested having a go at driving her car round the grounds, she agreed somewhat cautiously. In the event, it went very well, and Annabel enjoyed herself. It gave her back some confidence, which she'd been sadly missing of late.

'Thank you for my very first lesson,' Annabel said. 'I must say, I was nervous about being taught by Pettigrew — or even Lucas, for that matter.'

Jane laughed. 'Don't let any of them

bamboozle you. I know what you mean, though; men always seem so superior, especially so when it comes to driving. I think you'll make an excellent driver once you get to grips with the basics.'

Annabel looked unconvinced. 'I've decided I'm going to take lessons when I go back home. Somehow I'll have to find someone to babysit, though. I don't think it would be ideal having Thomas in the car, do you?'

'Definitely not,' laughed Jane. 'He's another male, after all.'

'I was wondering . . . I haven't seen Caroline Harker around. Is she away?'

'Not as far as I know,' Jane said, and smiled ruefully. 'Things didn't go too well at Christmas, you know. What with Jon being his impossible self, and Caroline doing her best to make Luke jealous . . . She's still angling to be the next Mrs Lucas Wylde, but I think Luke doesn't want to declare himself just yet. After all, it's not a year since Roxy died. It's far too soon for any sort of formal statement of intent.'

So that's how the land lies, thought Annabel. *Lucas is all but spoken for. Shame.* She thought she had more in common with Lucas than she did Jon, and he would have made a wonderful father to Thomas. But anyway, she wasn't ready to get involved — and wasn't sure if she ever would be.

18

Jane woke Annabel early one morning to say there was a fire at Seacrest.

'Oh, no!' she cried, leaping out of bed. 'What's happened? How serious is it?'

'Not sure,' Jane replied, still in her dressing gown and slippers. 'All they said was that there had been a fire, and it was being brought under control. I came to tell you straight away. Now, I'll go and get dressed, then I'll take you to see for yourself.'

Annabel hurriedly threw on some clothes and went to see that Thomas was all right. Rosie was already giving him his breakfast, and agreed to look after him for a while. Then Annabel went downstairs, where she met Lucas. He obviously knew what had happened, and insisted she join him for some breakfast before rushing off to

Scarborough. Jane arrived shortly afterwards.

'What a terrible thing to have happened,' Jane said, 'but it's a good job you were not there, that's all I can say.'

Annabel didn't know what to say. If she had been there, maybe it wouldn't have happened; but, on the other hand, it would have been dreadful if she had been trapped in the blaze ... She couldn't wait to see what the damage was. She forced down some toast and managed to swallow some tea, but was grateful when Jane said they had better be off.

Jane drove over-cautiously, Annabel thought, secretly urging her to put her foot down. She remembered that when she had been speeding about the grounds with Roxanne, she had been much more wild and careless. They arrived at last in Scarborough to find the road outside the house cluttered with vehicles; Jane was directed to a parking spot further down. Annabel leapt out of the car almost before it stopped, and rushed down the footpath, anxious to learn what had happened. A fireman halted her progress, but let her pass when he discovered who she was.

'Can you tell me if there is anyone living there now?' he asked.

'No,' she said immediately. 'It was empty. Only my son and I live there usually, but we've been away for a few days.'

'Fine. That's all we need to know.'

As the fireman turned away, she called him back. 'I know this may sound odd, but I thought perhaps you ought to know. Just before I left, I had the strange feeling someone had been in my kitchen, helping themselves to food. It might not mean anything, and I may have imagined it . . . '

'Why didn't you say something?' Jane asked looking horrified. 'Did you check all round the house before you left?'

'Yes — at least, I think I did. I was rather fearful it was my amnesia returning, I'm afraid, so I didn't take it too seriously. It was only some bread and cheese, and maybe some milk. Nothing of consequence.'

'Has anyone else got keys to your house?' the fireman demanded.

'Apart from me, just a builder I employ — Steve Johnson,' Annabel replied brusquely, 'and I trust him implicitly.'

As she said his name, Steve appeared at her elbow. 'Thank goodness you are all right,' he said. 'I couldn't believe it when I heard it was your house that was on fire. Any idea how it started?' he asked the fireman.

He shook his head. 'Too early to say, but there was no sign of forced entry.'

Annabel looked at Steve and saw his face turn white. 'Honestly, I had nothing to do with it, I promise you. When I left nearly a week ago, everything was hunky-dory. I haven't been back since.'

'Yes,' Annabel said. 'I know, because I was there, remember? I locked up myself.'

Steve frowned. 'You didn't see a sort of tramp at all, did you?'

Annabel shook head.

'One turned up while I was finishing off the cloakroom. Jack the electrician was with me. We were having our lunch break when this chap appeared at the back door. He said he was looking for Miss Broom. Apparently, whenever he was in the area, she used to give him the odd meal — at least, that was what he told us. Jack and I shared our sandwiches with him and made him a cup of tea, and that was the last I saw of him. I left him chatting to Jack. He'd gone by the time I'd finished packing up.'

'You don't think he was hiding up in the attic, do you?' Jane said with a shocked look on her face. She turned to Annabel questioningly.

'I suppose it's possible,' she said slowly. 'I can't remember the last time I checked up there. I can't believe someone would hide up there while we actually living in the house, surely?' She didn't sound too convinced.

'It looked as if someone had lit a fire in the living room,' the fireman said. 'That was where the most damage occurred, but the hall and staircase are also affected. We found a whiskey bottle on the floor in the kitchen, and the back door was wide open. I'm afraid the building will be declared structurally unsafe until a surveyor has inspected it.'

It was quite some time before Annabel was allowed to see the extent of the damage, and when she did, she was simply appalled. She felt like sitting down and crying. The building was quite uninhabitable in its present state. Jane agreed, and together they gathered what possessions Annabel wanted to take, before making their way back to the car. A very subdued Annabel arrived back at Chellow Hall to be greeted by Lucas, who immediately told her she was to stay just as long as she needed.

He was very attentive towards Annabel, much to Miss Caroline

Harker's consternation. She still made an appearance from time to time, and didn't take kindly to seeing Annabel so settled there. Annabel wondered if she should say something to let her know that she had no designs on Lucas, but could not bring herself to do so. Jane became more of her friend and confidante, and they laughed together about Miss Harker's snooty behaviour.

'What happened between you and Jon — if you don't mind me asking?' Jane asked one day as they sat by the fire.

Annabel shrugged her shoulders. Jane deserved to know the truth. She had been such a help since the fire, running her back and forth, and no doubt she would tell Lucas what she thought he needed to know.

'Perhaps I had better start at the very beginning. I'm not sure how much you know about me. My parents were killed in an air raid when I was twelve years old, having just started at the secondary school. The Palmers were near-neighbours, and very good friends. I often used to visit them, so when I became homeless they took me in and brought me up as their own.

'I was happy as one could be in the circumstances, and when I left school I got a job at the local library. I wanted to earn some money, and try to repay the Palmers for all their kindness. They really put themselves out for me, and I know it wasn't easy. When I turned twenty-one, I thought it was time I found a place of my own. That was when they produced a suitcase they had kept in the loft. They had forgotten all about it. It contained all that was salvaged from my old home. Well, to cut a long story short, that was when I discovered I might have a distant relative living in Scarborough.'

'Miss Broom?'

'Yes. I knew her as Aunt Agnes. She was a sort of aunt on my mother's side of the family, I believe. So I decided to take a holiday and see if I could locate her, just to say hello. I wasn't sure if she was still alive, but thought it would be nice to have at least one relative to send a Christmas card to if she was. I was wandering along the seafront at Scarborough wondering how to set about finding my aunt — it was proving more difficult than I thought — when I was almost knocked down by Jon. I'm not sure to this day whose fault it was. I may have absent-mindedly meandered off the path. Anyway, Jon invited me back here, introduced me to Sir Robert, and that was that.'

'So Jon bedazzled you, like he's done with so many girls,' Jane said with a laugh.

'Yes, I'm afraid so. I soon realised, of course, that he wasn't to be taken seriously; but he was most charming, and I was — *smitten*, I think the term is. We had a few laughs together, and he took me for a few spins in his car. I enjoyed his company, and I suppose I was a little in love with him, if truth be known. However, the night of Sir Robert's birthday party, I got rather tipsy. I didn't drink much normally — just the odd nip of sherry to be sociable — but I indulged in a few too many glasses that night. I began to feel light-headed, so Jon suggested I needed fresh air, and he took me out into the garden. We went as far as the summerhouse, and then we . . . well, I knew it was foolish at the time, but I didn't care. We got rather — carried away . . . '

'Oh, deary me. He's always been quite a trial for Robert. The trouble is, he's such a charmer.'

'Hmm,' said Annabel. 'Anyway, I didn't see Jon much after that, but I wasn't really surprised. The next thing I heard on the grapevine was that he was getting married to Patsy. I suppose you could say I was a mite disappointed, to say the least. Strangely enough, I didn't know I was pregnant until just before Christmas, when you suggested I went to see the doctor. It just shows what an innocent I was. I was in quite a panic, I can tell you. I simply fled back to

London.' She sighed. 'The Palmers were wonderful. I know they were terribly upset to start with, but when they got used to the idea, they rallied round and helped tremendously. I couldn't have managed otherwise.'

'I'm so glad you came back to Chellow, and I regret very much the part I had to play in sending you to Uncle Percy's. I never wanted that to happen, you know. It was all Roxy's doing.'

'I realise that, Jane. Don't forget, I know what Roxanne was like. She certainly led Lucas a dance.'

19

Jane had given Annabel a lot to think about. If what she said was true, both Luke and Jon were interested in her — or, should she say, interested in becoming Thomas's father? She rather thought Luke wanted Thomas because he wanted an heir. Did he really have romantic feelings for her? And Jon? Did he really love her, or was he simply interested in her inheritance? He was always short of funds, although perhaps that wasn't quite the case for the moment. She hadn't seen much of him recently. He said he was terribly busy with Patsy's business, but she rather suspected he was enjoying the position he found himself in, lording it over the staff at the hotel. Since Patsy hadn't made a will, he would inherit everything — much to Patsy's parents' disapproval, no doubt. *Why must life be so complicated?* Annabel wondered. All she wanted was to be left in peace to bring up her son.

Annabel had finally passed her driving test, and was now the proud owner of a small car. She was thrilled to bits by the freedom it gave her, and was exceedingly grateful for Jane's patient tuition. She was driving to Scarborough, having arranged to meet Steve at Seacrest to discuss the proposed renovations. The house was apparently structurally sound and ready for work to be done on it once again. Steve was already waiting outside when she drew up.

'Sorry; am I late?' she asked.

'Not at all,' he replied, locking up his van. 'I was early.' He looked a little downcast. Perhaps business was a little slow. She would soon remedy that. Annabel smiled to herself. She was delighted to see him, and knew that if she had brought Thomas with her, he would have been pleased too. She liked Steve's calm, sensible manner, and also his honesty. She felt she could trust him unreservedly, she didn't know why. Strange, how she felt unsure of Jon's integrity, and yet Steve she would trust with her life.

'Shall we go and review the damage?' she said, unlocking the front door. 'I think I've changed my mind about converting it into flats.'

'Oh?' was the only response from Steve as he followed her inside.

'Yes,' she said. 'I want this to be my home, at least for the time being. I want to bring Thomas here as soon as I can. I'm tired of — oh, I don't know. I just want to be alone with my son for a while. Give myself time to think.'

'The Wyldes getting to you, are they?' he asked, following her into the kitchen.

She turned to look at him. 'Sort of, I suppose.' He had hit the nail on the head. She did need some space from them for a bit. She wasn't happy, though, with Steve's demeanour. He was usually so lively, but this morning he looked as if he had all the cares of the world on his shoulders. 'Are you all right?' she said. 'You look a little sad today.'

'Could be better,' he replied.

'Anything I can do to help?'

He shrugged his shoulders and took out his notebook. 'Just found out my girlfriend has been two-timing me, so I'm a bit cheesed off. Now, what have you decided you want done as a priority?'

Sensing he didn't want to talk about his troubles, she pulled out a chair and sat down at the kitchen table. She had brought a flask of coffee and some sandwiches that she distributed straight away. 'I want suggestions.' She grinned. 'I'm not very good at this sort of thing, so I was hoping you would come up with some ideas for the whole place. I know it's asking a lot, but I desperately want to come and live here as soon as I can.'

'You want this to be a family home?'

She nodded. 'If this were yours, what would you do?'

He looked around and took a mouthful of coffee. 'Well, I think this kitchen wouldn't take much to sort out. It's superficial damage. The cloakroom fortunately wasn't touched, so the main area to sort out would be the room you use as a sitting room.'

She nodded her acquiescence. 'I quite agree. I know it's not what you usually do, but do you think you could do the necessary work for me? I'd help with some of the painting and so on, if you don't think I'll be in the way.'

He looked a little startled.

'I did help my adopted parents with decorating. I'm not completely useless. Actually, I think I would quite like to do some of the work myself. It would make it feel more mine.'

He laughed. 'You're the boss. Just tell me what you want, and I'll do it.'

'Have a sandwich,' she replied, and joined in with his laughter. 'I know it must seem strange, me having all this, and being able to buy whatever I need . . . but it wasn't always so. I'm not too comfortable with it yet. I suppose I've been overwhelmed at times by the grandeur of Chellow Hall, but I have come to feel that's sort of artificial in a way. I can't see me wanting to live that kind of life, and I do want Thomas brought up in a more suitable environment. Does that make sense, do you think?'

He nodded his head and smiled. 'Yes, I do understand. I couldn't ever imagine living in such luxury, with servants to tend your every whim.'

'It was a wonderful luxury in a way, but also I feel it's a wasteful kind of existence. I wasn't brought up to cope with that lifestyle. Now, what are we going to do with this house?' she said, gathering up the remains of the food. 'I would like a playroom for Thomas, and possibly a room for my books.'

'Well, there is no shortage of space. Are all the bedrooms to be on the first floor, then?'

'Yes, I think so. I'm going to spread out a bit. I've even thought of possibly employing a live-in nanny.'

'Good idea. She could have the attics, couldn't she?'

She nodded with a smile. 'Good idea. It will seem rather strange to begin with, but I think it is going to make sense. Especially if I have friends to stay. The house won't feel so large then.'

★   ★   ★

When Lucas heard that Annabel was transferring to Scarborough, he was very disappointed.

'I need to be there to supervise the work,' she told him. 'After what happened, I don't want it to stand empty any more.'

'I was hoping you would see Chellow Hall as your home, Annabel. I thought perhaps we could bring up Thomas together . . . '

'I'm sorry, Lucas — really, I am — but I don't think I'm the one for you.'

He looked downcast. 'I need an heir, as you know; and I thought Thomas was . . . '

'I don't think so,' she said quickly. 'I am grateful for all that you have done for me, but I do think Miss Harker would be far more suitable for you. I'm sure your father would agree, especially as you seemed to be getting on rather well together. I gather Miss Harker's parents were friends of your father's first wife.'

Lucas shrugged his shoulders. 'Yes, so I understand.' He sighed. 'So be it. Do I take it that you are in love with Jon?'

She shook her head. 'No. Definitely not. Besides, I haven't heard or seen anything of him since Patsy's funeral. I gather he's been busy with the hotel.'

'So he says,' Luke remarked cynically. 'However, he is expected home sometime next week I believe.'

Annabel noted this, and decided she would definitely be in Scarborough by then.

Rosie decided that she too wanted to leave Chellow Hall, and asked if Annabel would be in need of her services.

'If Lady Jane says it's all right, I would welcome your help looking after Thomas. Why do you want to leave, though? I thought you liked it here?'

'I like looking after children, and when you leave there will only be Sophie, but she isn't here all the time. Besides, I would like to be in Scarborough, where there is more going on during my time off. I'm hoping having Chellow Hall mentioned on my reference will help get me a better job in future.'

Annabel could understand that, and agreed to speak to Jane on Rosie's behalf.

★   ★   ★

Three days later, Annabel, Thomas and Rosie arrived with their entire luggage at Seacrest House. When Annabel showed Rosie the attics and asked if she would be happy living up there, she was over the moon.

'It's wonderful,' she declared. 'I promise I'll take good care of Thomas and be available at any time.'

Annabel was beginning to think everything was going to plan . . . until she introduced Rosie to Steve. They seemed to hit it off very well straight away — a little too well for Annabel's comfort. Now that Steve was fancy-free again he was perhaps vulnerable.

20

Seacrest House was rapidly taking shape. The downstairs rooms were all newly-decorated, and Rosie had made her rooms in the attics habitable. Steve worked long hours, for which Annabel was very grateful. When she quizzed him about what he did in his spare time, he just shrugged, and said *What spare time?* Obviously he hadn't made it up with his girlfriend, so seemed happy to work late.

Annabel began preparing evening meals, which they all had in the kitchen, and they discussed progress and ideas. It felt so cosy and normal that she knew she would be sad when the work was all completed. She had grown used to having Steve around, so much so that she wished he didn't just see her as an employer. She couldn't think of a way of letting him know how she felt, so they continued in the same easy-going fashion. At least he didn't appear to see Rosie as a substitute girlfriend, as far as she could tell.

* * *

Jon arrived out of the blue one day — primarily to see Thomas, he said, but spent most of the time explaining why he hadn't been around recently. He was full of his latest venture, looking after the hotel that he had decided to sell. He scowled when he saw Steve, and suggested he take Annabel for a walk, saying they had things to discuss in private.

Annabel agreed, largely because she didn't want any unpleasantness, so she grabbed her coat and said she could do with some fresh air. Scarborough was looking very beautiful in the warm May sunshine. Children ran in and out of the sea, squealing and laughing with delight. Annabel smiled when she envisaged Thomas doing the same in a few months' time.

'I know I haven't been around much recently, Annie,' Jon said, taking her hand as they walked along the seafront, 'but you must realise how difficult this has all been for me. Soon it will all be much easier, I promise.'

'Don't worry about it,' Annabel said. 'Thomas is being well looked-after, now I have Rosie helping me.'

'I don't just mean Thomas,' he replied. 'I want to see more of you too, Annie. In time, we can legalise our arrangement — after this blessed mourning period is over, of course.'

This stopped her in her tracks. 'How do you mean?'

'Why, we'll get married, of course. I gather you turned Lucas down; and besides, I am Thomas's father, after all. Luke wasn't the man for you, and I'm glad you realised that. He's far too serious, and I wouldn't want him taking over my son.'

Annabel chewed her lip. 'I don't know where you got that idea from, but

I have no intention of marrying you, Jon.'

He tried to laugh it off. 'Sorry, maybe I was a bit precipitous. Let's wait until the dust settles, eh? You've had quite a time these last twelve months, too. Mine hasn't been so easy either. We'll talk about it some other time, perhaps when you're not distracted by the work at Seacrest.'

'No, Jon, you're not listening. I have no intention of getting married — to you, or anyone else — just to give Thomas a father.'

He raised his eyebrows at her decisiveness and scowled. 'Do I have to fight you for custody of Thomas?'

She stared, horrified, then without another word simply turned on her heel and scurried back to the house. He called after her, but fortunately didn't pursue her. She was frightened as well as exceedingly angry, and by the time she arrived back at the house she was almost in tears.

'Are you all right?' Steve asked,

seeing her distraught face. 'Here, come and sit down. You look terrible. What's happened?'

'I'm all right,' she said, but slumped down on the settee by the fire and held her head in her hands.

'What's happened?' Steve asked again, cautiously.

'He's going to apply for custody. Because I said I wouldn't marry him, he's going to try to take Thomas away from me.'

Steve went to sit beside her. 'He can't, can he? Surely he wouldn't have a claim. Anyway, why would he want to?'

'Because, unless Luke has a child, then Thomas would be the Wylde heir,' she said bleakly.

Steve blinked. 'I see. So, what are you going to do about it? What *can* you do?'

'I don't know. I really don't know.'

★ ★ ★

Annabel spent a sleepless night considering her options, and the one she favoured most was marrying Steve. If she was married, she felt sure she would be able to counter any opposition from Jon. She thought she did actually love Steve, and so did Thomas. The only problem was: did Steve feel the same way? It was a big problem and one that needed resolving as quickly as possible — but how?

For the next few days, Annabel was very preoccupied and anxious. She pounced on the mail when it arrived, fearing a letter from the Wyldes' solicitor. She couldn't eat or sleep with the worry. Finally, Steve said he could stand it no more, and threatened to quit if she didn't calm down. Steve leaving would be unbearable, so she tried her best to behave more normally in his presence.

One day, Steve suggested she needed a night out. 'How about going to the pictures?' he said.

'I don't like going on my own,' she admitted.

'I would be happy to accompany you

if you like. Rosie will look after Thomas.'

Annabel was in a tizzy, not sure what to wear for her date with Steve. She changed several times before settling on a multi-coloured flared skirt and white top. She added a cardigan for later. She couldn't recall the last time she had spent so much time getting ready to go out — and they were only going to the cinema, for goodness' sake. *Pull yourself together*, she admonished herself.

It felt strange walking along the main street with Steve, now dressed in smart trousers and shirt. She had no idea what films were being shown, and to be honest, didn't much care. She was feeling much younger and more carefree than she had of late, and couldn't help but smile. Now all she had to do was get Steve to fall in love with her, and all would be well.

'Penny for your thoughts,' he whispered, seeing her grin.

Somewhat startled, she responded automatically, 'Not worth a penny.

Have you seen the queue? I wonder if we'll get in?'

'Of course we will. This is normal.'

Sure enough, half an hour later they were ensconced in seats in the circle just as the curtains went up.

Later, Annabel wasn't too sure if she could have explained what the film was about, but she had enjoyed it all the same. Steve had even bought her an ice cream during the interval. As they left the cinema, they automatically wandered down onto the seafront, where the fairy lights twinkled and the ocean gently swept the shore.

'This is lovely,' exclaimed Annabel. 'It's been ages since I had such an enjoyable time.'

'You're easily satisfied,' remarked Steve as they crossed the road. 'Don't you miss the bright lights of London? That is where you come from, isn't it?'

'Hmm. Yes, I was brought up in London by some friendly neighbours who adopted me when my parents were killed. They were not very well-off, but gave me a good home, for which I will always be exceedingly grateful. I've always been a quiet, studious person, so I didn't go out much. I didn't have the money, anyway; you know what it's like. A trip to the cinema on a Saturday night was the highlight of my week back then.'

'I heard you mention the Palmers before. When they came at Christmas, I thought they seemed like nice people. How come you ended up in Scarborough, then?'

Annabel paused before replying. It seemed strange he didn't know about her inheritance. 'I thought you knew. I came here to find my aunt, Miss Broom, but ended up working at Chellow Hall. As you may have gathered, I was seduced by Jon Wylde, and then had Thomas. When my aunt died, I inherited everything, much to my complete surprise. I still can't believe how wealthy I am. I just wish I had been able to meet her. I'd have loved to have met her, and to have known what it was like living at Seacrest in her day.'

'Wow,' said Steve. 'Quite a tale of rags to riches. I didn't realise.'

'Please don't let it make any difference to us,' she said earnestly. 'I've come to rely on you so much, I don't know what I would do without you.'

His eyebrows rose. 'That's very flattering, though I don't know if I deserve it. I'm an ordinary guy trying to make a living, that's all.'

Annabel smiled. 'I suppose, to start with, I was totally overwhelmed by the grandeur of Chellow Hall, and it's only now I realise that lifestyle isn't all it's cracked up to be. When I first went there to work, I thought how marvellous it all was. You know — the huge ornate rooms, the large staff, the extensive grounds . . . It was so different from what I had been used to, but gradually I saw the other side of the coin. The expense of maintaining such a property, the way the Wyldes behaved as if they were so much better than everyone else. I appreciate all they have done for me, don't get me wrong. I must admit they have been very generous and kind, but I can't see me living that sort of lifestyle, and it certainly isn't what I want for Thomas. I know that makes me appear ungrateful. I don't know what I should do.'

'I see your predicament. I suppose Jon Wylde would want to inflict all that on you, given half a chance.'

She nodded. 'I won't let that happen. Thomas is mine, and I want him brought up to value a more simple life like I had. Lucas Wylde obviously has the responsibility of looking after the estate, which I think he finds onerous, but I believe he enjoys it just the same; whilst Jon doesn't know what to do with his life. Now he has the hotel to look after, he may change — who knows?'

He took her hand as they continued along the seafront and gave it a squeeze. 'Let me know if there is anything I can do.'

Oh, there is, she thought, but merely smiled. 'Thanks.'

They continued to Seacrest House, and Annabel gave him a peck on the cheek before he left for home.

* * *

During the next few weeks, Steve took Annabel out occasionally, much to Annabel's delight; and fortunately she heard nothing more from Jon. She wasn't complacent, though, and fully expected he would be back to make further demands.

One Saturday, after Steve had finished work for the day, Annabel suggested he stay for lunch, and afterwards they could take Thomas for a walk on the beach. Steve had looked a little down, and she thought it might cheer him up. It was a pleasant afternoon, and Annabel smiled to herself when she thought they looked like a family. *Would that it was so,* she sighed.

Steve's thoughtful mood returned towards the end of their outing, so when they returned to Seacrest, she invited him in for a cup of tea. She did wonder if he had been thinking along the same lines as she had. Was he perhaps seeing her as more of a girlfriend? And, if so, what was the problem?

She quickly buttered some scones, and they took them into the newly decorated living room. She had just asked Steve what seemed to be bothering him when the phone rang. Annabel sighed and went to answer, annoyed by the intrusion, and came back looking pale and upset.

'Problem?' Steve asked, getting up to leave.

'I'm afraid so. That was Luke on the phone. Apparently his father has died.'

'Oh dear, I am sorry,' Steve said. 'Please let me know if there is anything I can do. I expect that means you will be spending more time at Chellow Hall again?'

She nodded, a bit distractedly, still stunned by the news. 'Jane will be devastated. I must go to her.'

21

Annabel didn't know what to expect when she arrived, but as the days went by she began to wonder why she was there at all. The Wylde relatives descended on Chellow Hall, and earnest discussions took place, all to do with the prospects of keeping the estate within the family. She heard snatches of conversations about the amount of taxes or death duties that would be demanded, and the gloomy faces wondering if it was the end of the line for the Wyldes at Chellow Hall.

Annabel tried to remain in the background, but assisted where she could, especially with Jane and Sophie. Having Thomas with her helped. They spent a good deal of the time in the nursery away from everybody. The day before the funeral, Jane found them there, and sat by the window quietly surveying the garden. Eventually, she sighed.

'I shall miss this, I know, but in some ways I will be pleased to escape. I suppose that sounds terrible, doesn't it?'

Annabel shook her head, but was a little surprised. 'No, of course it doesn't. I quite understand.'

'Do you? You know, when I first met Robert and we came to live here, I was totally overwhelmed by it all, but gradually came to find it somewhat oppressive. It was far more opulent than I had ever dreamed, of course. I came from an ordinary home in London, like you. It was because Robert wanted to remain here that I accepted it. I would have been happy to live anywhere as long I was with him. Now I can't wait to get away. It's all just too much.'

'Where will you go?' Annabel asked going to sit beside her.

'Spain,' she replied promptly. 'Robert and I were happy there at our villa, living a much more simple life. I only hope it is possible for me to keep it once the financial details are resolved.'

Annabel gave her hug. 'I shall miss you, Jane. You have been a good friend to me, and I hope you will keep in touch wherever you are. It's such a shame you have no family to help you through this.'

Jane smiled sadly. 'Actually, I have, but I lost touch with them when I married Robert. I think perhaps it's time I made my peace with them. It's funny how your views alter with different circumstances. I never thought I would be a widow before I was thirty . . . but then again, I never expected to meet and marry someone like Robert. He really was the love of my life, and I don't know what I will do without him.' She burst into tears again and sobbed on Annabel's shoulder.

When she had recovered her composure, Annabel said, 'I didn't know you had family alive. Are they still in London?'

Jane nodded. 'Yes, my parents live in the East End, and I have two sisters. Debbie will be twenty-five next month, and Babs is twenty-three. They are both married and have children of their own, but I haven't seen any of them for ten years or more.'

'Jane, I've just thought of something. Why don't we both go and stay at Seacrest with the children until you can make the necessary arrangements to go to Spain? I imagine there will be all sorts of legalities to deal with before you can escape, as you put it, but it might be easier on you if you were not here at Chellow Hall.'

'Are you sure?' Jane said eagerly. 'Would you really put up with us for a while?'

'Of course. It will suit both of us, because I feel like an outsider here at the moment; after all, I'm not family.'

'Bless you, Annabel. I always think of you as a Wylde for some reason. I think Lucas will be pleased to have the place to himself until he comes to terms with whatever the will throws at him. If I'm correct, he's going to find things exceedingly difficult, because I fear Robert left the estate divided between the two of them. Luke always understood he was to be the main beneficiary, so it will come a terrible shock, I think, to hear that Jon is to have half.'

Annabel rolled her eyes in surprise. 'Gosh, that will put the cat among the pigeons.'

Jane chuckled. 'Nothing surprises me with this family. Maybe Jon will be like a breath of fresh air and the two brothers can work together after all. Who knows? I just don't want to be around to hear the arguments.'

* * *

Annabel and Jane left the day after the funeral, and Seacrest became a more welcoming home with the two children to look after. Unfortunately, Rosie handed in her notice, saying she had been offered another post which she wanted to accept. Annabel didn't really mind, but could have done with a bit more time to adjust.

A few days later, Steve came by with his latest bill for work completed, and shyly told Annabel that he and Rosie were engaged. Annabel was somewhat taken aback, but did her best to congratulate him and say how pleased she was for them both. Now it was clear why Rosie wanted to leave. Perhaps it was for the best. Now that Seacrest was becoming more liveable-in, she could manage without Steve's services. Pity, really, because she had relied on him for inspiration, but now she would have to cope alone — or, at least, with Jane's assistance while she was staying there.

At Annabel's suggestion, Jane wrote and asked her family to visit. It was something she was nervous about doing, but since they ought to be told Sir Robert had died, it seemed only right to propose they meet. Her parents declined the offer, but her two sisters agreed to meet up, and actually arrived the following weekend. It was a wonderful noisy time once they got over their initial wariness, and Annabel could see it was just what Jane needed. She thought how wonderful it must be to have sisters to chat to, and it made her thoughtful about bringing up Thomas alone. She would love to have more children, but that would depend on finding a suitable partner. One thing was for sure: she wouldn't settle for anything but love.

She left the sisters alone for a while, saying she had promised to take Thomas to feed the ducks, and agreed to take Sophie along too. She had grown to love the lively little girl, who had become much more amenable since she had started school. Poor Sophie — it was hard for her to understand what had happened to her father. As she wandered along, she thought about the recent tragedies: first Roxanne, then Patsy, and finally Sir Robert. What a terrible amount of misfortune for one family. She hoped Jane would find peace and contentment in Spain.

22

'You really ought to have been there,' Jane said when she arrived back at Seacrest, looking flushed. She had been staying with Annabel since the day following the funeral to escape the numerous relatives who wanted to commiserate with her, so had accepted Annabel's offer of accommodation. Finally, the family had been summoned to the reading of the will, which Annabel had also been requested to attend. She had refused, she said, on the grounds of not being related to the Wyldes, and because she had no babysitter. She could have found someone to watch Thomas and Sophie, but really had no interest in what Sir Robert had willed to his successors. Somehow, it seemed money was just as much a problem when you had some as when you hadn't. She hoped Lucas and

Jon didn't fall out over the inheritance, whatever it turned out to be.

Jane looked shattered when she returned, and flopped down on the settee still in her outdoor clothes. 'You really ought to have been there,' she reiterated. 'It was dreadful.'

'Why, what happened?' Annabel said, handing her a cup of tea. 'Worse than you expected, I gather.'

'Far, far worse. I don't know how it will be resolved, so I'm glad I shan't be around to see the fireworks.'

Annabel sat down in the armchair opposite, and waited while Jane pulled herself together and had some tea. Eventually, Jane put down her cup, and settled back with a huge sigh. 'Fortunately, I have inherited the villa in Spain as I had hoped. I have been well taken care of, thankfully.'

'So?' queried Annabel, feeling curious after all.

'Well, after the staff had been rewarded for their long and dutiful service, it only left the estate to be dealt with. Everyone assumed it would be left to Lucas, of course.'

'And it wasn't?' Annabel said with raised eyebrows.

'No, and that's not the only trouble. Apparently, after death duties have been paid, there will just be the house and a few acres — including the stable block and the odd farm. The rest of the land and so forth will have to be sold off. It came as a shock to all of us just how much would have to go. Luke has made such a good job of managing the estate that it was worth more than we thought. Anyway, the family stared in disbelief when the solicitor announced it was to go jointly to Robert's sons, Luke and Jon — with the proviso that Jon and you got married, making Thomas his legitimate grandson. If Jon doesn't marry you, he gets nothing. Eventually, if there are no further legitimate male offspring, then Thomas will inherit.'

Annabel was stunned into silence.

Jane waited until she had taken in the

impact of what she had said before carrying on. 'Obviously you can't be forced to marry Jon, but it leaves him in a very difficult and somewhat embarrassing situation. I don't know why Robert did it, I really don't. As far as I knew, he had all but disowned Jon, but I suppose he was rather chuffed to think he had a grandson to follow on the Wylde tradition. He was, after all, of the old school that didn't think girls should have equal standing with boys. Poor Sophie doesn't count. Thank goodness she's not old enough to care one way or another.'

'I'm pleased you got what you wanted,' Annabel said with a genuine smile. 'You deserve to relax in the sun. I know you always said how much you enjoyed the villa. Sophie does too, doesn't she?'

'Oh yes, we will be fine. Robert, bless him, made sure we were provided for; but I'm worried on your behalf, Annabel. Whatever will you do?'

'I just don't know. I never expected

any mention in the will at all. You know that. I'll have to consider what is in Thomas's best interests, won't I? I'd welcome any suggestions,' she added with a sigh, and went to see what the children were up to as it had been rather quiet for the last few minutes.

★   ★   ★

Annabel expected Jon would contact her before long; but, as it turned out, it was nearly a week later before he rang suggesting they meet somewhere for a quiet chat.

'Of course, Jon,' she replied softly, 'we do need to talk, don't we? Jane told me about the contents of the will. I presume that is what we have to discuss?'

★   ★   ★

Two days later, Jon collected her from Seacrest and drove them to the hilltop overlooking the town. Here he pulled in and switched off the engine. 'This do?' he enquired.

She nodded her agreement. It really didn't matter where they were, although the view was stupendous.

'I'm so sorry about all this, Annabel. It certainly isn't of my doing, you realise? I don't know what my father was thinking about.'

'Yes, of course. I do understand. I gather from Jane that the will states you need to marry me to inherit your share of what remains of Chellow Hall. Is that correct?' She wanted to be sure, and not discover Jane had been mistaken, although it was highly unlikely.

He nodded. 'In a nutshell, yes. I am still having difficulty in getting my head round it. Firstly, though, I have to tell you that I really don't need Father's money. That's not the issue here. I'm concerned about Thomas. It might not matter to him at the moment, but perhaps it may in the future.'

'What will you do if I don't agree to marry you?' she asked, not wanting to be bamboozled, but seeing his line of thinking and realising he had a point. Thomas would always have the stigma of being illegitimate if she didn't marry.

Jon shrugged. 'What I intended to do anyway. I'm going to buy Chellow Hall from Luke and live there — run my business from there. Now I have the funds, having sold the hotel, I can pursue my own ideas. Whatever you decide has no bearing on my position; I'll just have less money to play with. Poor Luke's already decided he's had enough of the hassle and wants a quieter life. In time, I expect he'll marry Caroline and settle to life as a county gentleman, but first he intends going on a cruise to help clear his mind of all that has happened in the past year or so. It was my suggestion, and he's agreed to have a holiday before making any major decisions. I do not intend to contest the will, by the way, and neither does Luke. Father's wishes will prevail, at least as far as we are concerned.'

He took hold of her hand and kissed

it. 'You, sweetheart, will have to make up your own mind. I would be delighted if you would do me the honour of becoming my wife, but it has to be based on the right reasons. Don't you agree?'

'Yes, of course,' she agreed readily. 'I've done nothing else but think about it for the past week, and unfortunately I'm no nearer a solution. You know I think a lot about you, Jon. I care for you a great deal, especially as you are the father of my child, but I won't be rushed into a marriage of convenience for you or anyone else. As far as I'm concerned, marriage is for keeps, and isn't something to take on lightly. All that concerns me now is Thomas.'

'I totally agree. I know in the past I have made huge mistakes, so I haven't got a good record . . . but honestly, Annabel, that is all truly in the past. There will be no more gambling or wild partying. I mean to make my son proud of my achievements.'

23

Jane and Sophie left for Spain a few days later, promising to keep in touch and hoping Annabel would visit them soon. 'A few days in the sun would do you a power of good,' Jane said, giving her a warm hug. 'We are going to miss you terribly.'

'I shall miss you too,' Annabel said, close to tears. 'Take care of yourselves.'

Next to leave was Lucas, accompanied by Caroline, who had managed to book a cruise at short notice. Caroline seemed to be a highly organised individual, and clearly intent on becoming the next Mrs Wylde. *Lucas had better watch out*, thought Annabel; although perhaps Caroline was just what he needed. She had a social standing in the local community, and was a lover of horses: seemingly an ideal companion for Luke.

It seemed as if everyone wanted to escape to collect their thoughts, but Annabel felt she needed to remain at Seacrest and have some peace and quiet alone with Thomas. So much had happened in such a short space of time. She needed to re-evaluate her life and decide what her priorities were. Seacrest, though, was too quiet and a little overwhelming. While Steve had been busy working there and Rosie had her rooms upstairs, it had felt more comfortable, but now it didn't feel quite so homely as she imagined it would. She did consider going to see the Palmers, but that was not an ideal solution. She had to find a way of being content with her life — alone.

On fine days, she took Thomas for walks round Scarborough and along the beach, even paddling in the sea occasionally. Thomas loved being on the beach, and enjoyed the donkey rides and ice cream. He was easily pleased. At night, once she put Thomas to bed, Annabel had time alone with her thoughts — which went round and round as she wondered what she ought to do.

She was delighted when Jon phoned to ask if he could call to see them at the weekends, as he was now on his own and finding Chellow Hall too quiet. Most of the staff had now left, and only the Peterses and various gardeners remained. Nobody was sure what would happen in the future, but one thing was certain: it would never be the same again. Chellow Hall, everyone admitted, needed to be brought up-to-date and run on more modern lines. It seemed there was general agreement that with some money spent on it, it could be run far more economically, and with fewer staff too. Jon was busy setting up his livery stables and organising riding lessons, along with managing what was left of the estate, so it would appear that, no matter what Annabel decided, he was going to be running Chellow Hall from now on — albeit along different lines to what had happened in the past.

Annabel felt she had lost her momentum and inspiration with her plans for Seacrest, but she was fascinated with what Jon had planned to do at the Hall. He seemed so enthusiastic, and she found she enjoyed the time she spent with him. She looked forward to the weekends. Jon was easy to get along with, and didn't put pressure on her to marry him. They enjoyed a pleasant, friendly relationship. But she was startled one day when Thomas began calling Jon *Dada*. Was her son helping her make up her mind?

What began as one lovely day out turned into a disaster of momentous proportions. Annabel had driven to Whitby intent on buying some flowers to place on Sir Robert's grave, as requested by Jane before she left. The town was reasonably busy, but fortunately she had no problem parking right outside a florist's shop. Thomas had fallen asleep on the back seat, so Annabel decided to leave him there while she popped into buy the flowers. It would only take a minute, so wasn't worth disturbing him. He'd had a poor night, and was a little bit grumpy — possibly teething, she thought; but if he didn't seem any better later, she intended to take him to the doctor.

There was only one other customer, so Annabel picked up a bunch of freesias — her husband's favourites, Jane had told her — and idly glanced out of the window at her car. She hoped Thomas was all right, poor little soul. He seemed a little feverish and generally out of sorts. She was a little worried about him, and wished Jane was there to discuss it with her. Finally, the assistant was ready to deal with her, and seemed to take such an inordinately long time processing the change and wrapping the flowers up that Annabel was becoming anxious. She didn't like leaving Thomas too long in case he woke.

Finally, she managed to extricate herself from the garrulous assistant, and fled outside — only to stare in stunned horror at the discovery that her car had disappeared. She wildly looked all around, desperately trying to recall if she had set the handbrake. But the car couldn't have rolled away as it was a perfectly level road. No, someone had taken it. Someone had got into her car and driven it away with her son on board! She felt faint with worry, and started to scream.

The shop assistant took hold of her arm, propelled her to a nearby chair, and asked if she was all right. Annabel gasped for her to call the police and say her car was missing. Who would do such a thing? Who would deliberately kidnap her son? *Maybe they didn't notice him*, she thought. But what would they do when he woke up?

'Can I call someone to be with you?' the assistant asked. 'You really need someone . . . your husband maybe?'

Annabel shook her head, but then decided Jon needed to be informed. He would know what to do. She only hoped he didn't castigate her for leaving Thomas in the car unattended; she knew now it had been a stupid thing to do.

He arrived very quickly and took charge, demanding to know what was being done to find their son. He spent some time talking to a constable before helping a distraught Annabel into his car, saying the police would contact them at Chellow Hall as soon as they had any information. He was obviously as upset as she was, but managed to remain calm, which helped. She explained between sobs about Thomas being asleep, and why she hadn't locked the car. She had left the windows open so Thomas wouldn't get too hot . . . She would never forgive herself if anything happened to him.

The next few hours were a nightmare. She couldn't keep still, and kept thinking about her son — alone with strangers, feeling bewildered, miserable and hungry. It also made her think about the future: if anything should happen to herself, who would look after Thomas? She hadn't made a will, so there was no provision for him — but then she had never in her wildest nightmares considered such terrible events taking place. When she looked at Jon's strained face, she knew with sudden clarity what she had to do. Thomas needed two parents in his life, and he loved Jon just as much as she did; she should never have doubted it. Jon had changed from the irresponsible rascal he had been when they had first met, into the caring, sensible man he was today. He had coped with her tears and overwhelming outbursts of misery so rationally. She felt so scared and immature by contrast.

* * *

Three hours later, the police phoned to say her car had been located and Thomas was being brought to Chellow Hall. He appeared to be unharmed, they said, but was understandably upset

— and demanding an ice cream. Annabel was so relieved he was alive and well that she would have let him have anything he asked for. She and Jon hugged each other with relief.

'Thank you, Jon,' Annabel said, slumping down onto the settee. 'I don't know what I would have done without you. Sometimes, when I look at our son, I feel so inadequate — it is such a huge responsibility bringing up a child, and I just want to say that I am truly grateful for all your help today.'

'That's what fathers are for,' he said, with a grin and another hug. It seemed he couldn't take his arm away. 'I'll always be there for you, Annie. I know how you feel, though. Parenthood is quite a responsibility, and I hadn't really appreciated that until now. I want to help in any way I can with Thomas's upbringing; you can count on it. So, whatever you decide, I'll go along with. I love you.'

She sighed, and then quietly said, 'I've done a lot of thinking, and this may not be conventional . . . but how about if Thomas and I move in here with you for a while? Just to see how it goes. And if, in a few weeks, we seem — how shall I say? — compatible, then perhaps we should get married and give Thomas his birthright. That is, if you still want to.'

'That sounds like a wonderful and extremely sensible idea. I do like the sound of it, and I have all sorts of things I want your help with, so you need never be bored, I'll make sure of that,' he added with a chuckle. 'One thing I hope you will want as much I do, Annie — if we do get married, I want more children to bring Chellow Hall to life. I don't want Thomas to be an only child leading a lonely, solitary existence. Do you agree?'

'Yes,' she said with enthusiasm. 'Yes, yes, I do. I want lots of brothers and sisters for him. I was an only child, as you know, and for the most part quite happy. But I do feel I missed out on family life.'

'Annabel, my darling, you make me the happiest man alive. You are just perfect.'

'I don't know how to tell you this, but . . . well, I think I have always loved you, but . . . truth to tell, I'm scared.'

Jon instantly took her hand and gave it a squeeze. 'Whatever it is, just tell me, and let's sort it out. I'm sure we can resolve it. What is worrying you?'

She sighed and stared at the fire, unable to face him. 'The thing is, I've never been with a man, you know, apart from when we . . . You must think me a complete idiot.'

'My darling Annabel! If that is all that concerns you, then you have nothing to worry about. I promise you, we will take our time, and only do what pleases both of us. Being good friends comes first, and then it's only what comes naturally, I do assure you. So please don't worry on that account. As I said before, if you agree to be my wife I shall be the happiest man alive. With you by my side, I believe we could work wonders around here, and have a great marriage. So, what do you say? Will you take pity on me and marry me, sweetheart?'

'Yes,' she said shyly. 'I'd like that very much.'

*　*　*

It was to be a quiet wedding at the local church with just a few relatives and friends, so Annabel was stunned by the number of well-wishers that turned out. Jane returned from Spain so Sophie could be a bridesmaid, and also to look after Thomas while the newlywed couple had a short honeymoon. Lucas and Caroline, looking refreshed after their holiday cruise, made a point of wishing Annabel all the very best. Annabel hoped Caroline caught the wedding bouquet. Lucas seemed so much happier and relaxed as he told her he was house-hunting, hoping to find something suitable not too far away. Annabel guessed there would be wedding bells in the not too distant future for him and Caroline, and hoped they would be happy wherever they settled down.

Mr Palmer looked embarrassingly proud as he led Annabel down the aisle, but pronounced himself pleased as Punch at being asked to give her away. Mrs Palmer had a tear in her eye as she told Mrs Peters, sitting next to her, that Annabel was truly beautiful, just like her mother.

Annabel held her head high as she walked beside her new husband, down the aisle and out into the autumn sunshine. *I've done it*, she thought, with a smile on her face. *I'm now Mrs Jon Wylde, Mistress of Chellow Hall, and our son Thomas will inherit everything*.

We do hope that you have enjoyed reading this large print book.

Did you know that all of our titles are available for purchase?

We publish a wide range of high quality large print books including:
Romances, Mysteries, Classics
General Fiction
Non Fiction and Westerns

Special interest titles available in large print are:
The Little Oxford Dictionary
Music Book, Song Book
Hymn Book, Service Book

Also available from us courtesy of Oxford University Press:
Young Readers' Dictionary
(large print edition)
Young Readers' Thesaurus
(large print edition)

For further information or a free brochure, please contact us at:
Ulverscroft Large Print Books Ltd.,
The Green, Bradgate Road, Anstey,
Leicester, LE7 7FU, England.
Tel: (00 44) **0116 236 4325**
Fax: (00 44) **0116 234 0205**

CHRISTMAS AT CASTLE ELRICK

Fenella J. Miller

Severely injured in the Napoleonic Wars, Sir Ralph Elrick has been brooding in his castle for years, waiting for Miss Verity Sanderson to reach her majority and marry him. The week before Christmas, she sets off to his ancestral home to become his wife. But Castle Elrick is a cold, unwelcoming place — and Ralph and his small staff are not the only residents. Will Christmas be a joyous celebration, or will the ghosts of Castle Elrick force the newlyweds apart?

THE ROSE AND THE REBEL

Valerie Holmes

In stifling summer heat, Miss Penelope Rose decides to take a swim
— scandalously, in an outdoor pool
on her father's estate. Having sent
off her maid, Penelope strips to her
underclothes and indulges herself in
the coolness of the secluded water.
But when she climbs out, wearing
only her soaked chemise, her dress
has disappeared! To make matters
considerably more embarrassing, she
finds herself standing face to face
with the culprit — Mr Lucas
Bleakly, the eligible bachelor son of
the local reverend . . .